Secrets in
PARIS

ANN EL-NEMR

Jan-Carol
Publishing, Inc

"every story needs a book"

Secrets in Paris
Ann El-Nemr

Published November 2019
Little Creek Books
Imprint of Jan-Carol Publishing, Inc.
All rights reserved

This is a work of fiction. Any resemblance to actual persons, either living or dead is entirely coincidental. All names, characters, and events are the product of the author's imagination.

ISBN: 9781950895267
Library of Congress Control Number: 2019954619

You may contact the publisher:
Jan-Carol Publishing, Inc.
PO Box 701
Johnson City, TN 37605
publisher@jancarolpublishing.com
jancarolpublishing.com

To all the women that have learned to survive
and start a new life.

Dearthie
I thank you for being there
when I needed you.
You are the best at your
craft. I hope this book
take you away from all
your worries and to
another world though's
least for a few hours
Always! Enjoy!
Dr. S. Dom
2022

Letter to the Reader

This book is centered in one of my favorite cities of the world: Paris. This story will make you feel as if you are visiting the many beautiful sights as my characters explore the city and the country-side. Many conclusions came to mind while writing this book, so I pondered before I decided a sequel had to be written to finish it. Marcia will take you into a world most people cannot even imagine. What she had to do to survive will shock you. Now, that she has a shameful past she wants to keep hidden, she travels to Paris so she can start a new life. She cannot resist Stephane's charm nor his love, but unforeseen danger lurks around the corner. You must under-stand, everyone has skeletons in their closet, so what would you do if someone was going to expose them? Marcia's choices may surprise you. Enjoy!

Yours truly,

Ann El-Nemr

Chapter 1

It was a rainy day in mid-August. A young woman walked quickly, taking long strides down a crowded walkway as her heartbeat pounded in her chest from nervousness, or maybe adrenaline. Her head held high, she stared straight ahead, avoiding everyone's eyes. She wore a Burberry black trench coat, palazzo pants, and black Louboutin high heels. She carried a large bag over her arm. Her eyes were hidden by a pair of black sunglasses, and her shoulder length blond hair bounced with every step she took. Her hips swung from side to side as she made her way through the alley. Men turned their heads to take a second peek at her while wishing she belonged to them or wondering who she was.

Keep walking. Don't stop until you get to the gate, or you might not go. No, this is your destiny, your dream. Keep walking and don't look at anyone. You can do this, she kept telling herself over and over again.

She arrived at the Air France boarding gate and stopped near the counter, leaning against one of the walls. She was at Terminal E at Boston Logan Airport. She waited with anticipation for her one-way flight to Paris, never looking at anyone. She dropped her carry-on bag next to her leg, then took her boarding pass and her American Passport from her pocket to verify her seat again. She noticed her hands were trembling, so she placed them, along with her papers, back in her pockets as she counted the minutes to board the plane. Her eyes closed momentarily, and she bit her lower lip, taking a deep, impatient breath as she tried to calm herself. She was about to make a life-changing decision. *I hope I'm doing the right thing and that I won't regret this choice later*, she thought. *What if I don't like Paris? What if... Stop it! You will be just fine. You can always come back.*

Marcia Philips was a beautiful woman in her late twenties. She was an only child, orphaned. She had lost her parents in a car accident caused by a drunk driver while she was in her sophomore year of college. She had been pursuing a business degree at Bentley University in Boston, Massachusetts, and had always dreamed of opening her own high-end clothing store and being her own boss, but her aspirations had been shattered by the pain that enveloped her at that time. She was now alone. Since her parents had both been schoolteachers, they had not been able to save much money while trying to put her through college. They had left her a small bungalow, which she sold for nearly nothing in order to pay for the funeral cost and the pile of hospital bills that was left behind after their death. Tears pooled in her eyes every time she thought about them. It had been a difficult few years trying to cope with their passing and reorganize her life to survive. She had worked two jobs to try to continue her studies, but it had been very stressful balancing both work and college. Many nights she had lain awake in bed, wondering how she was going to pay the rent or her tuition. She had been waitressing at a diner in the evenings and tutoring other students on campus, but she had still been having difficulties meeting both ends...until that one late afternoon when she had met Tiffany. That seemed like such a long time ago, an eternity, but it had only been four and a half years earlier.

A year had passed since the death of her parents. Marcia sat at a table, her hand under her chin, in the library of the university. Her table was by one of the windows, and she gazed at the blue flowers outside. She was wondering how she was going to finish her schoolwork on time and still manage to get to her waitressing night job at seven, and then she was interrupted. Out of the corner of her eye, she noticed someone standing by her table. Marcia turned her head and looked up at the girl, giving her an annoyed look. A tall, lean girl in her mid-twenties stood motionless, her long black hair tied up in a messy bun. Marcia noticed her stunning blue eyes. She was dressed in blue jeans and a gray Bentley sweatshirt, and she was glancing down at Marcia.

"Hi, do you mind if I sit with you? There aren't any other empty tables by the window, and I like the sunlight," she said as she set her backpack on the table and then processed to pull the chair back. She sat down on the chair before taking her accounting book and her computer out.

Marcia stared at her, frustrated at the disruption, but answered, "Sure, go ahead," in a flat tone. Then she directed her attention back to reading her business assignment.

"My name is Tiffany Reynolds. You're in my accounting class with Mr. Brown, aren't you? I've seen you around campus," the girl quietly said as she took a pen out of her pencil case, seemingly preparing for her studies.

Marcia casually looked away from her book, curled her lips at the girl, and nodded, irritated at being bothered again. "Yes. I don't mean to be rude, but I need to finish my project. I don't have time to chat," she told her firmly, then returned to staring at her computer screen.

"I'm sorry to intrude, but I was told that you're really good with numbers. I heard you tutor other students on the side for extra cash and that you are the best around, so I thought maybe you could... Listen, I really need help, and I can pay you whatever you want," she replied.

Marcia watched as Tiffany tilted her head down, cast her eyes away, and shrugged her shoulders in desperation. She pressed her lips together, trying not to burst out laughing at her expression, but she couldn't keep herself from smiling. Although it would take time away from her own studies, she needed the money. She looked at the clock on the far wall, then grinned at Tiffany and nodded her head.

"My name is Marcia Philips. My fee is fifty dollars per hour. I only have an hour before I have to go to work. What do you need help with, and what don't you understand?" Marcia asked her.

"Everything!" Tiffany answered, and then they both laughed. From that day on, they became best friends, and Marcia's life changed forever.

Marcia was brought back to reality when she heard the flight attendant at the counter announce her flight number. She lifted her head and noticed people getting in line at the first-class row. She bent down, gripping the handle of her bag tightly. She exhaled heavily as she took a couple of steps forward to get in line behind the other passengers who were boarding the first-class section on the plane. She took her passport from her pocket and opened it so she could look at her boarding pass, glancing at her seat number again: 3A. The line started to move forward, and she slowly made her way to the airbus that was going to take her to her new life. She quickly arrived at her assigned seat and set her bag down, opening it and taking a magazine out, and then she stored her carry-on in the overhead storage compartment. Slipping off her coat, she gave it to the flight attendant so she would hang it up in the closet, then thanked her. She placed her pillow and blanket to the side and sat down while she waited for the other passengers to board.

"Would you care for anything to drink?" another attendant came by and asked her.

Marcia looked up at her and shook her head. "No, thank you. I'm all set," she answered.

She reached down for her seatbelt buckle and fastened it around her waist, then made herself comfortable by putting her pillow behind her head and wrapping the blanket around herself. She prepared for the long flight overseas. She didn't want to eat, watch television, or talk to anyone; all she wanted to do was sleep until she landed in Paris. Her head was hurting, and her whole body ached from lack of sleep. She was rubbing her temples with her fingers when a feeling came over her that someone was observing her, so she slowly turned her head to her left to look. A well-dressed man in a tailored suit and tie sat in the seat next to her, just across the aisle. She watched him as he loosened his tie and then placed his hands on his knees, all the while focusing on her. *Hmm! Handsome*, she thought. He was in his early thirties. A strand of his dark brown hair had fallen on his forehead, but it was his deep aqua eyes that made him intriguing. From how intensely he stared at her, it was almost as if he could read her mind. He never uttered a word. Their eyes locked for a few seconds, but it seemed like longer, and then he smiled, showing her a perfect set of teeth. Marcia didn't move or return his smile. She was instantly brought back to why she was leaving Boston and how easily it would be to engage him into conversation for her benefit, but she was done with that lifestyle. She didn't need a man in her life at this moment. She angled her face away from him and sat back in her seat, hiding behind the panel of her pod so he couldn't see her.

She closed her eyes, hoping sleep would invade her soon so she could forget the events that had burdened her over the last four years, but it was not to be. Her thoughts went back in time, reminding her why she was flying across the world and trying to forget those days. She was determined to put her life back together, without any drama or men.

Tears formed behind her eyelids as she thought about what she had done to survive, what she had done to be able to move forward and finish the last years of college. She balled her fists under the blanket as she tried to wash away the horrible memories. *Don't do this to yourself,* she thought. *It's over. You are a strong, independent woman, and you need to put the past behind you and move on with your life. Focus your energy on achieving what you have yearned to do since you were a little girl. Learn about fashion and be a successful entrepreneur. Time will heal all wounds. Leave the past behind and concentrate on the future.*

She shook her head, trying to dismiss the bad memories that still haunted her. She felt the movement of the airbus under her as it took off down the runaway, headed toward France. Fifteen minutes later the plane was in the air, and she couldn't turn back now. Less than a half hour later she had reclined her seat into a bed, and she was sound asleep.

* * *

The mysterious man sitting next to Marcia on the plane was Stephane LaRoche. He was the heir to a large vineyard in the region of Epernay, located northeast of Paris. For many years his family had produced some of the best award-winning wines and champagnes in the world. He was being groomed to inherit one of the most prestigious plantations in France, called LaRoche Vineyards, which yielded the best grapes used in winemaking. Stephane and his younger sister, Etienne, had been taught every aspect of the industry since they had been children. They were meant to take the over the business and bring it to the next level in the world of wine awards. Stephane's father, Michel, was to pass over the reins of the company to Stephane after his retirement later that year.

While in line to board his flight, Stephane stood a couple of passengers behind the woman with the black trench coat. He had followed the blonde with his eyes as she walked past him and headed to the first-class section of the Air France flight. He was enthralled by her for some unknown reason, and he hoped he might get to meet her on the seven hour trans-Atlantic flight. He loved the way she held her head high with confidence, as if she was in control, walking with a bounce in her stride. He even loved her manicured fingernails. Everything about her aroused his interest. He hadn't seen such a beautiful woman in a long time. He desperately wanted to see her eyes, which were hidden behind those black shades.

How in the hell can I like this woman so much? She hasn't even spoken a word to me! This is totally absurd. She is probably married, or she at least has a boyfriend, Stephane thought as he followed behind her. He felt joy when he found out his seat was next to hers. He glanced down at her left hand as she passed her coat to the flight attendant—no wedding ring. He walked to his seat, never taking his eyes off of her, and quickly sat down. He placed his briefcase down next to his feet, then buckled in. A sexual rush passed through him as he realized how close he was to her. If he reached over the aisle, he could touch her. *I bet her skin is as soft as silk*, he thought. He had to know more about this woman. He couldn't move, and he hoped she would look his way. Unable to stop himself, he stared at her. Never in his life had something like this happened to him. It was as if he was drawn to her. He watched as she placed the pillow behind her head before unwrapping the blanket and spreading it over her body. He rubbed his hands together nervously, undoing his tie and then placing his hands on his lap, all the while keeping his eyes on her.

For God's sake, stop it! Stephane's mind screamed. *She's only a woman. You have had hundreds of them over the years. What's so different about her?* he asked himself. But he was attracted to her like no other.

Stephane was pleased when she leaned forward in her seat and glanced his way. *How beautiful she is!* His heart skipped a beat as his eyes met hers, so he smiled her way. She held his gaze for what seemed like a long time, and lust invaded his being. He was about to introduce himself to her, but she turned away before a single word was said. She moved backwards and disappeared behind the partition of her seat. Stephane's shoulders slumped forward, and his heart sunk as he realized that he had failed to capture this woman's attention. Never in his life had that happened. He leaned back in his seat, disappointed. *Maybe I'll have another chance later*, he thought.

He stayed awake during the whole flight by watching a movie, reading contracts, and having supper, but while he did all of that, she slept. He got up to use the washroom twice, just so he could spy on her. He strolled the aisle slowly, admiring her from afar as she slept. As he stopped by his seat and looked over at her, he saw that she was on her side, her blanket covering her up to the shoulders. He could see the curve of her hip and her untidy hair, which was caused by her tossing and turning in the confined space. She looked so peaceful. *I need to calm myself. This is ridiculous! Never have I wanted to meet a woman in the way I do now*, he thought to himself, taking his seat quickly so she wouldn't catch him observing her sleep.

He peeked over toward her seat every time she moved, hoping she would sit up and he would be able to talk to her, but she slept through the whole flight, and the flight attendant had to wake her up right before the plane landed. He watched her fold her blanket, pull a bottle of water from her bag, and take a sip of the water. He kept tapping his fingers on his knee nervously. His heart began to beat faster at the anticipation of talking to her. He still couldn't see her face. She finally stood up, turned her back to him, and bent down to grab her pocketbook. His eyes were locked on her. He pulled himself to the edge of his seat in the hopes that he might be able to help her with the carry-on that was surely in the overhead compartment, but she just walked down the aisle toward the washroom without even looking his way. He leaned over his armrest and observed as her hips swayed from side to side with every step she took. He sat back in his seat, disappointed, but he wasn't going to give up so easily. He kept watching for the red light from the bathroom to turn green, as it would give him an indication that she was coming toward him again.

Stephane waited patiently until he saw her come down the row. She had fixed her hair and put on red lipstick. *Wow! How I would love to kiss those lips*, he thought. He shifted his body closer to the side so he could see her better. Her head was facing to her right, away from him, as she walked back to her seat. She was only ten feet away. She was going to sit down again, and he would lose his chance to talk to her. *Do something to get her attention. Say something before she sits down again*, he kept repeating to himself.

Chapter 2

Marcia opened the door of the bathroom and then locked it behind her. She stood with her hands on the small counter, bowed her head, and exhaled deeply. She had not dared to look the man's way. She saw how he had looked at her from the corner of his eye as she got up, and the only thing she could think to do was turn her back to him. *How is it that this man has had such an effect on me? Yet I don't know anything about him...except how handsome he is. But I need to concentrate on my plans to begin a new life. I can't be bothered with a man now,* she thought to herself.

She lifted her head up to examine herself in the mirror, and she gasped. She was horrified at how she looked from sleeping through the whole flight, but at least she felt rested and ready to conquer the world. Her hair was all over the place, and her makeup needed touching up. She opened her bag and pulled out her brush, then ran it through her hair several times. She applied red lipstick to her lips and smoothed her shirt with her hands. *Much better! Now, get going and stay away from him,* she told herself.

She was about to head back to her seat, and she had a feeling his eyes might be on her again, so she was going to do everything in her power to avert him. She held her head high, pushed her chest out, stood with her back erect, and struck the pose she had been taught by her friend Tiffany. She went around the cabin corner and looked away from him. Every stride she took was well calculated until she arrived and gracefully slipped into her seat. She reached down for her buckle and snapped it on. Then she heard his voice. She knew it had to be him. He had a French accent, so smooth and sexy. She couldn't help herself and looked up at him.

"Is there a line for the washroom?" he asked her casually as he stood by her seat, one of his hands on the top of her seat and the other pointing toward the area at the front. She could smell his cologne, a musky scent, but it was the smile he gave her that was making her melt with desire.

"No, no line. I believe it's free. The green light is still on. It's all yours," she replied as calmly as she could while pointing to the indicator up front. She didn't smile or show she had any interest in him. She just bent down and placed her bag at her feet as if she was preparing for the landing.

"Well, thank you so much," he said politely. She glanced up and gave him a quick nod of the head. He patted her headrest lightly and nodded at her, his smile now gone, and then he walked toward the front. *You are so rude and bitchy when you wake up*, she thought. *He was only being nice, and you snapped at him. Next time be pleasant, will you? He meant no harm.* She grabbed her magazine from the side table, opened it, and began to scan through the pages.

"Flight attendants, prepare for landing," she heard the pilot say over the intercom as the stewardesses came down the aisles for their final check. She noticed that the man was walking back to his seat.

She grabbed her sunglasses and put them on. She bent her head down and pretended to be engaged in her magazine, casually turning the pages. *Keep going. Don't stop*, she told herself. She clenched her teeth and closed her eyes, and heat rushed up to her face at the thought that he might talk to her again. But he didn't.

Minutes later they were on the ground, rolling down the runway and then stopping at the gate. "Welcome to Charles de Gaulle Airport. The correct time is eight o'clock in the morning. Enjoy your stay in Paris," she heard the flight attendant announce.

Marcia unbuckled, put her magazine away, and stood up quickly to retrieve her bag from up above. She took a step back and accidently stepped on the man's foot as she tried to pull her carry-on from the compartment. She momentarily lost her balance, falling backward, so she grabbed the seat for support, but then she felt a gentle hand on her waist, which put an end to her fall.

"I'm so sorry! Pardon!" she immediately said, heat rising to her face from embarrassment. She looked down at his foot, but then looked back up at him as he pulled his hand away.

"No problem. Let me help you with that," he said, then pointed at her bag, which was halfway out of the compartment. She nodded at him and gave him a small smile. She moved to the side as he took her bag out, and he placed it on the floor in front of her, blocking her exit.

"Thank you," was all she could muster to say when he grinned at her. She gripped the handle of her bag and pushed it forward toward the exit. She wanted to say something else to him; however, she was tongue-tied from embarrassment, and nothing came out. The line started to move, to her relief. She never looked back, although she knew he was close by, as she could still smell his cologne. Marcia hurried her pace in the direction of immigration and the customs line for non-citizens. Only then did she dare to take a glimpse over her shoulder. She saw him in the French citizenship line. A sigh of relief came over her when she realized he wasn't next to her.

Marcia proceeded through immigration and customs without being asked too many questions. She continued down the escalator and headed to the baggage carousel, where she flagged down a porter to help her pick up her luggage and wheel it outside. They headed toward the exit of the airport. A chauffeur was supposed to be waiting for her to take her to her destination. She stopped at the entrance to look for her driver. Many chauffeurs were standing in line and holding papers with names of clients on them. She was distracted momentarily when she saw the man from the plane once again. He greeted another man in a suit with a handshake, then chatted with him momentarily. He looked so professional and confident in his blue tailored suit, white shirt, and striped tie. He suddenly turned around and started walking in the direction of the entrance, exactly where she was standing. She froze. *Oh God! He's coming toward me. Where is my driver?* she thought. She tightened her grip on her carry-on. She scanned the area for her chauffeur or for her name on one of the signs, but she couldn't find either. She could hardly keep her eyes off of him, but she quickly took one last look his way, then turned away from him. He was still approaching her and was only a few yards away from her now.

"Miss Philips, I found your chauffeur," she heard her porter say. He was pointing at a man who was standing by the door and holding a card with her name written on it. She felt relieved. All she could do was nod at her porter. It brought her back to reality, and her façade was back on. She was about to take a step forward when she heard the man's voice again.

"Bonjour again, Mademoiselle. Can I offer you a ride somewhere? Andre, my chauffeur, could drop you off anywhere you need to go. It would be my pleasure. I can take a taxi into the city," he offered her. He stood inches from her, waiting for her answer. She could smell his fragrance again, and it was driving her crazy. It sent a warm feeling down her back. She already knew the answer to his question. She lifted her chin and looked straight at him.

"That's very gracious of you, Monsieur, but I'm all set. I already have a ride, but thank you so much," she told him, giving him a smile. Then she took a step around him and walked away, going to greet her own chauffeur.

But the man blurted, "Then maybe I could invite you for dinner this evening?"

Marcia stopped cold in her tracks and took a deep breath. She was surprised by how forward he was being as well as by how much she wanted to say yes, but she knew it was impossible. She gripped the handle of her bag tightly. She turned her head over her shoulder and took one last look at the handsome man, from head to toe then said, "I appreciate the offer, but no thank you." With long strides she walked away from him, leaving him standing at the doors of the entrance. She never looked back.

* * *

When Marcia rebuffed his invitations, he couldn't move. Time stood still, and he watched her walk away to greet her chauffeur.

Stephane's heart sank, and sadness invaded him. Never in his entire life had he wanted to know a woman as much as wanted to know her. *What happened? Who is she? Where is she going? What did she like or dislike about me? Why didn't I persist?* he wondered as he watched her get into the car and drive away. He was shocked and couldn't move. Women usually accepted his advances. He had never desired a woman as much as he did her. The only clue he had about her was that her name was M. Philips, which he had seen on the sign the chauffeur was holding.

"Sir, are you ready to go?" his personal chauffeur asked quietly.

Stephane nodded and whispered, "Yes, Andre. Let's go."

He walked to his car, disappointed. He took another look around before getting into the sedan, hoping to catch one last glimpse of her, but she was gone. Andre placed Stephane's luggage in the trunk, then came to sit in the driver's seat so he could take Stephane to his Paris apartment. Stephane sat in the back of the sedan for the forty-five minute ride from Charles de Gaulle Airport to Paris, the woman's image still stuck in his mind. His eyes became heavy from the lack of sleep from the flight, so he closed his eyes and rested his head back against the headrest. But all he had on his mind was that exquisite woman with the blonde hair, whom he hadn't been able to capture.

At the age of thirty-five, he still hadn't found the right person to fall in love with, because most women he encountered already knew who he was—a wealthy, single bachelor with old money and ties to the elite families of Paris. He was very proud of what he had accomplished since he had become the CEO of the vineyard. He had worked diligently for the last twenty years, ever since he had been a teenager. He had built the family company and made it twice as profitable in the last few years, and he had expanded the LaRoche Empire worldwide. But he still wasn't a happy man. He had a void he needed to fill. For years he had secretly been searching for the right woman to share his life with, to fill the emptiness he felt every night when he entered his apartment. He didn't have anyone there to greet him or love him, except the usual sexual partners, which he knew were dead ends. He had money, status, friends, and work, but he wanted more. His mother was a wise woman. Over the years she had told him many times to slow down and settle down.

"Stephane, mon amour, you need to find a good woman so I can have grandchildren to spoil before I die. Always remember that work will be there tomorrow, but it will never bring you happiness. Go and have fun. Go find a wife and be happy. That's all I ask," she had told him one night after dinner while they were sitting outside, finishing their glasses of wine, and staring at the view of the fields of grapes that lined the back of his parents' estate. She had smiled at him before kissing him gently on the cheek.

"I know. I love you, Maman," he had answered, and then he had placed his arms around her and given her a kiss in return.

That evening he had stayed outside after she had gone to bed. He gazed at the stars, and the wind blew warm air against his face as his mother's words echoed in his ears. She had been right. It was time for him to be whole and to fill his heart with joy.

Now he dozed off for half an hour while going down the highway, but the noise of the city streets woke him. He opened his eyes and looked out the window. They were already going down Peripherique Boulevard to connect to Sevre Street, near where Stephane had bought a condominium three years back. He had purchased a place there because he traveled back and forth from Epernay, where his parents lived, to downtown Paris for business. It was an extra two hour ride to the family estate. He was tired of hotel rooms, and it was very convenient for his needs when he stayed in the city. He loved the metropolitan lifestyle.

Finally, Andre parked the car in the courtyard in front of Stephane's building on Raspail Street. Stephane stepped out of the car.

He walked the short walk to the elevator that would take him up
to the fourth floor. He knew Andre would not be far behind him
with his luggage. His parents would always send Andre to help him
when he returned from a long trip abroad. Stephane could manage
without him, but he did appreciate his assistance. His condominium was a spacious place with several bedrooms and baths, and it
offered modern amenities for comfortable living. It had tall ceilings
and many long, glass windows, which allowed sunshine to warm
the rooms, but the feature Stephane loved the most was the large
balcony. It housed a table and chairs, which he used of the mornings as he drank his coffee and read the Le Monde newspaper. Every
morning he would sit there while admiring the view of the Square
Boucicault and Le Bon Marche in the distance. He loved to watch
people go by. It was the only hour of the day when he would put his
feet up, relax, and admire the Parisians as they walked down below.

He dropped his keys on the side table in the entryway and
proceeded toward his bedroom. He took his jacket off and threw
it on the chair next to his bed. Then he walked to the bathroom,
undressed, and took a quick shower. After drying himself off, he
walked naked back to his bedroom and lay down on his bed. He
needed a few hours of sleep before his day started. He closed his eyes,
the portrait of the unknown woman still on his mind.

* * *

Marcia sat in the backseat of the car in silence. Her head was
turned toward the window as she admired the sights of the newly
found city that she was going to live in for the next year. They drove
through the narrow streets of Paris and past the Eiffel Tower as they
followed the River Seine, heading to her new home. As the driver

drove down Saint-Germain Boulevard, her thoughts went back to the handsome Frenchman who had asked her to dinner. *Maybe I should have accepted. What harm would it have done? He was so pleasant toward me*, she thought. *It would have been nice to know someone in the city. No, you are not here for romance!* She wanted to explore the city without being interrupted by a man, especially one she didn't know.

The driver drove onto a narrow street named Madame Street, where she would be renting an apartment for the next year. The landlady was to meet her in front of the building at ten o'clock. She glanced at her watch and saw that it was almost that time. The car stopped in front of two red doors, and standing in front was a woman in her mid-fifties, dressed in a green dress. The chauffeur opened Marcia's door, and she stepped out of the car.

"Mademoiselle Philips?" the lady asked, a smile on her face as she stepped forward to greet Marcia.

"Yes, and you must be Madame Poirier. Nice to meet you," Marcia answered, extending her hand to her. They shook hands.

"Same here. Welcome to Paris! I hope you had an enjoyable flight and that you are not too tired. If you will follow me, I will show you your apartment so you can get settled in," the landlady kindly said.

"Thank you," Marcia answered as Madame Poirier opened one of the red doors with a key. Marcia followed her, and they walked up the stairs to the second floor, then down to the end of the corridor to the last door.

"This is it!" she said. They entered, and Marcia immediately loved the bright rays of sun that were coming in through the tall windows.

"This is a one bedroom apartment. It is a bit small compared to American standards, but it is clean, and you have a nice terrace that overlooks the street down below," she informed Marcia as she pointed to the basic amenities of the apartment.

"I love it. It's very quaint. Just what I was hoping for," Marcia answered excitedly as she followed the landlady around and examined everything. The furniture was a modern blue, and there were a couple of tall windows with yellow curtains. There was also a full bath with a laundry room. The kitchen was tiny, but it had a nice counter where she could cook. But then again, she was alone.

"And this is the bedroom; it has a large closet. I live downstairs on the first floor, so if you ever need anything, don't hesitate to ask. Any questions?" the lady asked, then passed Marcia two keys, one for the red front door and the other for her apartment. As Marcia was going back down the stairs and moving toward the living room, she noticed that the chauffeur had placed her suitcases by the door and departed.

"No, I really love it. It's perfect! Thank you," she said, answering the landlady. Marcia couldn't wait to unpack her things and find her way around Paris. Madame Poirier nodded, smiled, and then left her alone. Marcia locked the door behind the woman, turned around, and took another look at her new home.

A few hours later she had emptied her belongings from her suitcases and gotten familiar with the surroundings of her apartment. It wasn't a big place, but she adored it. "I suppose I need groceries if I'm going to eat," she said out loud to herself as she opened the cupboards in her kitchen. *That's the first thing I will do tomorrow morning,* she thought. Her stomach growled; she was hungry. She unzipped her carry-on and took out a bag of nuts she had bought at the airport on her way in. She popped a handful in her mouth. She felt tired and yucky from the long trip. She looked down at her clothes, which were wrinkled from sleeping on the plane. She walked to the small bathroom next to her bedroom and turned the hot water on. *A hot bath will relax me*, she thought.

Marcia sat down on the edge of the bed and undressed, letting her clothes fall to the floor. She hummed an Adele tune in her head as she returned to the tub, grabbing a towel from the rail next to the tub and placing it close by. She slowly immersed her body into the tub and exhaled, letting the warm water envelop her weary bones. It was only late afternoon, but she was ready for bed. She closed her eyes and soaked her body for an hour, just relaxing and listening to the outdoor noises of the birds, mixed in with the sounds of the faraway traffic.

Finally, she stepped out of the bath and dried herself off. She decided to go straight to bed so she could get up early the next day. She pulled the covers of her bed back and lay naked under the blankets. She shut her mind off and smiled, pleased with the decision she had made to move to Paris. She turned over to her right side, tucked her hand under her pillow, and fell asleep within minutes.

Chapter 3

Two weeks had gone by, and Stephane still had thoughts about the woman on the plane. It was as if she was haunting him every day. *I should have persisted. Maybe she would have accepted a date with me,* he thought. He sat on his apartment terrace, sipping his espresso and reading his newspaper. His feet rested on the chair next to the table. The one thing he loved to do was relax and watch people stroll down the street in the early hours of the morning, before his business day got hectic with meetings. He kept peeking over at the square, but his mind became distracted by a familiar figure as he looked down toward the walkway. A blonde woman in a pink summer dress was holding a straw basket and sauntering down from the avenue. He dropped his newspaper on the table and sat up straight. He focused his sight on the woman approaching the entrance of the square. His mouth dropped open, and his eyes widened in shock.

"It's her! Oh my God! It's her," he whispered out loud.

Stephane pushed his chair backward, letting it fall to the ground as he sprinted inside, veering toward the direction of his bedroom so he could grab his shoes. He put on the first pair of loafers that he saw and began running toward the exit. He picked up his apartment keys from the table by the door, then locked the door behind him. He didn't have time to wait for the elevator, so he bolted down the hallway and then down the stairs as fast as he could, holding on to the railing so he wouldn't trip. He burst through the front door, stopped on the sidewalk, and then raced across the street, not paying any attention to the cars going by as he rushed toward the square. His eyes scanned the area as he tried to find the woman in the pink dress, but he couldn't see her. He was panting by the time he reached the plaza.

Dear God! Did I imagine her? I must be wrong. I must be insane to run after a woman I don't even know. Maybe it wasn't her. No, it was her. How could I ever forget her? he thought. Stephane kept walking forward toward Le Bon Marche, his eyes searching every path, every woman he passed. His heart was beating hard against his chest, and he hoped he hadn't lost her. She wasn't in the square area; otherwise he would have seen her. He had crossed the whole area. As sweat dripped down his temples, he stood motionless at the other end of the square, at the busy streets where Le Bon Marche Galleria and La Grande Epicerie were located. He turned his head to the right, then to the left. He didn't spot her. But he didn't move. He had to decide which store she might have gone in.

There was no other option. But what if he chose the wrong store? Stephane knew he might never have another chance to see her again. *Think! She had a large basket, so she was probably going to the market for groceries.* He crossed the street quickly and headed for the main doors to the grocery store. He grasped the handle of the door and pulled it hard, entering the store. He took a few steps forward and scanned the large vegetable and fruit area. *Relax! Look! Search!* His eyes surveyed the place as he strolled slowly down the aisles and tried to catch his breath. All he could see were rows and rows of produce. Suddenly his heart skipped a beat. There she was, standing by the berries. He couldn't move, so he just stared at her from afar for a minute. He watched as she tilted her head and moved her hips as she wandered from one counter to another. He studied how she would choose and then examine each fruit before placing it in her cart. *She's perfect*, he thought.

Stephane pushed his fingers through his hair, then straightened his shirt. His hands were shaking from nervousness. *This time I'm not going to give up so easily.* He thought about what he was going to say to her for a moment. He absolutely wanted to get to know her, and he needed to have the right words. He held his breath, his sight glued on her as he took the first steps toward her. He picked up a red, plastic basket from the floor as he approached her. He threw some random fruits in it. She had her back to him. Her hair was tied in a ponytail, and before he could help himself, he examined the curves of her neck. He was four feet from her. One more stride, and he reached over with his hand and chose an orange, then placed it in his basket. He was so close to her that he could smell her floral fragrance. She turned her head slightly toward him as he looked at her. She had a surprised look on her face.

"Bonjour, Mademoiselle. So we meet again," he said to her as smoothly as he could, but she didn't say a word. She just stared at him, so he continued, "How are you enjoying Paris?" he asked then smiled at her.

"Good morning. I'm having a great time," she answered, then took a step away and moved toward the next aisle, ignoring him. He wasn't going to let her escape this time, so he followed her.

"You shop here often? You must live close by?" he asked as he randomly picked up fruits and put them in his basket, but she didn't answer him.

"My name is Stephane LaRoche. What's yours?" he asked, although he remembered her name was M. Philips from the sign her chauffeur was holding at the airport. He extended his hand to her, and she looked down at his hand nonchalantly, but she didn't shake it, so he pulled his hand away, disappointed. He longed to touch her.

"My name is Marcia. Now, if you'll excuse me, I have to finish my shopping," she told him. Then she moved a few feet away from him, ignoring him, but he wasn't going to give up so easily this time.

"Marcia, nice to finally know your name. I would love to show you the sights of Paris or take you out to dinner if you'll let me. I don't bite, and I'm polite. I'll be a perfect gentleman," he said, trying to make her laugh. He was watching her every move, and then he saw it. The corners of her mouth turned upward. However, it didn't last long; it vanished as quickly as it came.

She lifted her chin up, pulled her shoulders back, and said, "It's very kind of you, but no, thank you," and then she turned and walked toward the next aisle. His heart sank. A feeling of dread came over him. He had to try one more time. He wasn't going to let her go now that he had found her again, so he followed her.

"Okay then. An espresso at the café across the street?" he pleaded, but his appeal was rebuffed as she shook her head and continued walking away without even looking at him. She left him standing in the aisle as she disappeared around the corner. He was devastated and desperate to know more about her. He put his basket down on the corner of one of the tables, disappointed but not defeated. He wasn't used to being refused by women. He decided he would wait for her to finish her shopping and walked back to the main entrance where she had entered the store, hoping she would exit this way. He stepped outside in the fresh air. He crossed the street, head bowed low, and sat down in one of the chairs at the café that faced the doors of the store. She had to come out of those doors sooner or later. It was the main exit. He ordered an espresso when the young waitress came to his table. He crossed his ankles, folded his hands on the table, and waited for his drink as he kept a watchful eye on the doors of La Grande Epicerie.

A few minutes later the server placed his coffee in front of him on the table. He immediately took five euros from his pocket and gave them to her. He thanked her and sipped his drink. Forty minutes later she still hadn't come out yet. He looked at his Rolex watch for the third time. *Where is she? How long can it take to get groceries?* he asked himself. His foot began to tap against the ground impatiently, but his eyes were not going to divert from those doors, even though lots of people walked around the area.

Suddenly Stephane sat upright. *There she is!* He bowed his head and shaded his face with the menu so she wouldn't notice him. He peeked over the top of the menu. Marcia was coming out of the doors carrying two bags, one in each hand, and she turned right down Sevres Street. *Don't stand up right away. You don't want her to spot you,* he thought. He turned his head toward his right. Her back was to him. He stood up, then patiently waited for her to be half a block away before starting to follow her. *She has to live close by, or she would have taken a taxi,* he thought. He watched as her hips swayed from side to side and her hair moved in the wind. *This is ridiculous. If she sees me, she'll never go out with me. It will be the end.* She led him down Saint Germain Boulevard to an apartment building with a red door. He stopped and leaned against a neighbor's doorway, hiding from her in the archway of a building halfway down the block. He peeked to see what she was doing. She took her keys out from her pocket, opened the door, and disappeared in the edifice. Stephane grinned. At least he hadn't gotten caught. He now knew where she lived. He retraced his tracks to return to his condominium, all the while thinking about how he would see her again. He would find a way to convince her to at least let him take her to dinner.

* * *

Marcia was stunned when she saw him standing beside her at the supermarket. What a coincidence! She was speechless for a moment when she saw his azure eyes. He was so handsome and polite, but she knew where it would lead in the end. She was not prepared for any relationship. All she wanted was to be alone so she could concentrate on her career, visit fashion shops, and experience the Parisian flair. She didn't need a man. *Then why am I thinking about him again? Maybe I should have given him a chance? NO, NO, NO!* She had walked away as fast as she could. Thank God he had finally left her alone. Now she unpacked her things and put them away.

Her mind drifted to the day her friend Tiffany had come to visit, only to find Marcia crying in her dorm room because she wasn't going to be able to pay her tuition that month.

"Marcia, please don't weep. You are a beautiful woman, and there are a lot of ways to make money if you want to learn. I can teach you," Tiffany said calmly, placing her hand around Marcia's shoulder trying to console her.

"What are you talking about?" Marcia asked as tears rolled down her cheeks, naïve of what her friend was talking about.

"Get up right now! Stop sobbing and stop feeling sorry for yourself. You're young and beautiful! Now come with me. If you are willing to learn and keep an open mind, I will teach you how to make money. It might be difficult at first, but in time you will become a pro," Tiffany told her confidently, taking Marcia's hand in hers.

Marcia washed her face, and that day, Tiffany introduced her to her employer, the CEO of an elite private escort service for lonely, wealthy men. From that day on, Tiffany educated her on how to put up a facade, showing her how to flirt, how to dress, how to make men desire her, and, most of all, how to utilize all of her assets to gain the attention of rich men. She was outraged and disgusted at first, but as time went by, she adjusted to the life.

She never forgot her first encounter. She was so afraid of what might happen that her whole body was shaking. But he was gentle. He was a nice, lonely widow, and he just wanted to spend a couple of hours with a woman. Tiffany had handpicked him for Marcia. Afterward, Marcia hid in the bathroom and cried. When she came out, he was gone, but he had left her a tip of one thousand dollars on the bed. From that day on, she knew what she had to do to survive.

She benefited from their generosity until she graduated from college, and then she walked away from the lifestyle with a large bank account. It had been tough in the beginning, but she learned what needed to be done.

Stephane LaRoche. His name is so French. She kept repeating his name over and over as she walked back to her place. *Now, why did you dismiss him? You know you liked him...but he's just another affluent man. You don't need a man like that in your life. You'll only get hurt. You've seen it happen a hundred times with the girls you worked with. Rich men love you and then drop you for the next woman that comes along*, she told herself. She felt a little sad, but he was gone again, so she knew she just needed to forget about him. However, he was still on her mind when she entered her apartment. She placed her bags on the table and began to put her fruits and vegetables away in the refrigerator. She needed a distraction from that man. She glanced at the pile of papers near her stove. They were pamphlets of tours. She had picked them up while visiting the sights of Paris.

She seized the basket in her hand and brought it to the counter, where she placed each pamphlet in front of her. She decided to get out of the city for a couple of days and explore other parts of France. One brochure caught her attention—a small town outside of Paris called Epernay, about 120 kilometers northeast of Paris, in the hills south of Reims. It was famous for being one of the biggest champagne producers of the world. "Yes, that sounds like a fun place to visit!" she whispered. She gathered the other destination pamphlets together and dropped them back into the basket for later references. Her next move was to book a hotel and bus tickets. She decided to stay a couple of night so she could explore the town. She opened her laptop and began her search. She scrolled through numerous hotels until she finally decided on Hotel Villa Eugene, located in the heart of the town, on Avenue de Champagne. She took her American Express from her pocketbook, typing her card numbers in for a reservation at the hotel and for a bus ticket. She would be leaving in the morning on the 8:36 bus, which would arrive an hour and twenty minutes later. *Perfect! A change of scenery will do me good*, she thought, closing her computer.

Marcia rose from her seat and walked to her bedroom, where she took her Louis Vuitton carry-on from her closet and laid it on her bed. She unhooked two cotton dresses from her closet, removing shorts, a few blouses, and one pair of jeans from the hangers. She folded them neatly and placed them in her bag, then walked to the bathroom to retrieve her toiletries. She spent the rest of the afternoon singing songs and relaxing around her apartment. She forgot about the man with the blue eyes.

The next morning she woke up early. She called a taxi to take her to the Paris-Gallieni international bus station. On her way out the front entrance, she noticed a bouquet of at least two dozen red roses that had been delivered, but no one had claimed them. There was no card. She bent down next to them while waiting for her cab, smelling their fragrance. She was astonished that no one had collected them from the entrance. A horn sounded, and she looked up and saw that it was her taxi. She picked up her bag and walked to it.

By mid-morning she was in Epernay. She had enjoyed the scenic view along the way. When she arrived at the terminal, Marcia found a taxi stand and gave him the address for where she was staying. She was dropped off at a magnificent 19th century house that was once owned by the Mercier family and renovated into an upscale villa. It had been newly modernized to accommodate fifteen luxury rooms. She walked in and was in awe of the flowered gardens, the original chandelier, the high ceilings, and the spectacular décor. She checked in at the front desk, then walked up to her room on the second floor. She was storing her things away when she heard her stomach growl. She was hungry. There was a restaurant in the hotel; however, she preferred to find a tiny bistro where she could sit on a busy street and watch the bystanders. She went down to the lobby to talk to the concierge at the front desk.

"Bonjour, Mademoiselle. How may I help you?" the man in a brown suit asked her.

"Bonjour, Monsieur. Could you recommend a bistro where I could have lunch, preferably one where I can sit outside?" Marcia asked as she looked at the brochures that were displayed in front of her, which showed a variety of tours of vineyards in the area.

"Absolutely. If you walk down Avenue de Champagne and head to Loraine Street, you will find several restaurants and boutiques. Just take a left at the top of the street," he answered, then smiled her way.

"Merci! Can I take a few of these?" she asked, pointing at the leaflets on his desk.

"Yes, indeed. You must visit one of the wineries. It's very interesting and a lot of fun," he told her.

"I'll do that tomorrow. Merci," she told him as she stored a few in her pocketbook. She strutted out the front door in search of a place to spend the afternoon. She admired the Parisians as she strolled down the street. *They are so unique, and I love their accents,* she thought. At the end of her walk, she found a restaurant called Bistrot le 7, and she sat down at one of the tiny tables outside. She ordered an onion soup with gruyere cheese and a glass of white wine. She observed the Parisians go back and forth in front of her. Opening her bag, she took out the brochures about the vineyards and began to read the information. Her meal arrived soon after. Marcia picked up her spoon and enjoyed every bite. She returned to her reading after her stomach was full, and she sipped on a latte. She decided that she had to take a least one tour while she was in the region. The one she found most appealing was a winery that had been family owned for many generations. They were very famous for their exquisite champagne awards. It was called LaRoche Vineyards, located only a few miles from Epernay. She took her phone out of her purse and dialed the number from the brochure. Minutes later she had booked a tour.

She smiled to herself. After lunch she browsed the boutiques along the avenue for a few hours, then returned to her hotel and got ready for bed. She retired early, thinking about the exciting day of wine tasting that awaited her in the morning.

Chapter 4

Stephane sat at the edge of his chair outside on his terrace and sipped on his espresso, as he did every morning. This morning he kept scanning the street and the plaza attentively for Marcia. He was hoping to see her again. He looked at his phone on the table. Nothing! He wondered if she would call to thank him for the roses and tell him that she would go out to dinner with him. After he followed her home yesterday, he had mentally marked down her address. The minute he had arrived home that afternoon, he had picked up the phone to call his florist, ordering two dozen red roses to be delivered to her address.

The note had read:

Happy to have met you again!
I would love to show you the sights of Paris.
Please call me: 331-288-7666
Stephane LaRoche

It had been almost 24 hours since he had sent the roses, and he still hadn't heard from her. He grabbed his phone and dialed the number of the florist. He tapped his fingers on the table as it rang.

"Bonjour, Les Belles Fleures," the flower shop owner answered.

"Victor, this is Stephane LaRoche. How are you?" he asked as he kept his eyes on the avenue.

"Bonjour, Stephane. I'm good. How can I help you today?" he answered politely.

"Well, I was sitting here pondering whether you had delivered the flowers I ordered yesterday," he said, immediately anticipating the florist's reply.

"Oh! Yes, I did, but since I didn't have the number of the apartment and the landlord wasn't home I even checked the listing of occupants at the door, but no one by the name of Marcia Philips was indicated—I left the flowers in the foyer area. I figured someone would see them and know who she was. That was all I could do with the information you gave me," he said in an apologetic tone.

"Thank you, Victor. That's all I can ask," Stephane answered, then clicked the phone off. His heart sank. He would have to return to Epernay later this evening if he didn't hear from her. He had meetings at the vineyard tomorrow. He bit his lower lip, then sighed heavily, disappointed that the florist hadn't given her the flowers directly, but there wasn't much he could do other than be patient and hope she would receive them. He decided to wait by the phone another hour before jumping into the shower.

The afternoon passed slowly while he kept an eye on his phone and the square below, all the while reviewing contracts. By four o'clock he stood by the door of his patio, his hands on his hips. He took one last look at the square, then he bowed his head and shook it. *It's not meant to be. It seems that once I like a woman, she doesn't want to have anything to do with me*, he thought. He turned on his heels and walked into the foyer of his condominium, where his packed suitcase awaited. "Let's get going, Andre," he said quietly. His chauffeur took the suitcase to the car for the two hour ride home to Epernay. He bent down, grasped his briefcase, and opened the door, locking it behind him. He couldn't stay in Paris anymore, as his parents had called him several times and asked why he was still in Paris an extra week later. He had lied. "I'm exhausted from the long trip and want to relax a little. I'll be home soon," he had told his mother. He took the elevator down to the entrance of his building, then went out the door. With three long strides he was sitting in the back of his car, on his way back home.

"Andre, do me a favor. Could you drive down Madame Street? I would like to check something out," he asked him as he buckled his seatbelt and turned his face toward the window.

"Absolutely, Monsieur," Andre answered, a puzzled look on his face as he glanced at Stephane in his rearview mirror. He took off toward the destination without saying another word.

Stephane carefully observed the people strolling up and down the street. Hoping to see Marcia. His eyes scanned every pedestrian on the sidewalks as he searched for his special lady, but no luck. She was nowhere to be seen. The street of her apartment was just around the corner. Andre turned right on the street.

"Andre, pull over on the side of the street, just up here, please. This will be fine," he told him. Andre nodded. Stephane unbuckled his seatbelt and sat at the edge of his seat. His hand was on the handle of the door. He didn't care what happened; he just knew he had to see her again. He had never been lured to a woman in the way he was to Marcia.

"Here, in front of this building," he instructed Andre, pointing to her building. The car stopped by the curb. Stephane opened the car door and jumped out. He stepped in front of the red door and studied the names on the plaques so he could find out which doorbell to ring, but her name was not written anywhere. One of them said manager, so he pushed the button and waited for the door to unlock. A minute went by without a reply. He pressed it again. He began to fidget as he anticipated seeing her again.

The door swung open, and he faced an older lady. She was dressed in a beige summer dress, and her hair was pinned up in a bun. He smiled at her.

"Bonjour, Monsieur. May I help you?" she questioned him. Her hand was still holding the door.

"Bonjour, Madame. I am looking for Marcia Philips. Her apartment number was not indicated on the panel. Would you know where I could find her?" he asked pleasantly, hoping she would be able to help him.

"I'm so sorry, but Mademoiselle Philips is not here. I saw her leave with a valise this morning. I do believe she was traveling somewhere. I can leave her a message if you wish," the Parisian woman said.

"Would you know where she went?" he asked as he looked past her shoulder into the entryway, seeing the vase of red roses sitting on the ground, his flowers withered by the sun. He realized she had not received them. His heart sank. He returned his attention to the woman.

"No, I do not know where she was traveling. Anything else, Monsieur?" she answered.

"No. No, thank you, Madame. Have a good day," he told her, taking a step back as she closed the door. He stood on the sidewalk alone. He had lost her once again. He looked up at the rod iron balconies of the edifice, wishing she would be there waving down at him. He returned to his car, dissatisfied and frustrated that he hadn't succeeded. He sat in silence and mused over where she could have gone.

"Shall we go, Monsieur?" he barely heard Andre say. His driver waited patiently for his reply. Stephane nodded and closed his eyes, trying to picture her. It was hopeless. He sighed heavily. He needed to concentrate on his work and forget this woman.

"Yes, Andre. That will be all. Let's go home," he mumbled. He felt the car move forward, but this time he never looked back. He opened his briefcase, took out a contract brief, and began to read as they left Paris to return home.

A little over two hours later, Andre was driving down the private road that led to Stephane's family plantation. A fence adorned the driveway to the main house, with fields of endless green grapevines beyond. The main villa was a large, luxurious residence with green shutters made of limestone, a brown ceramic tile roof, and a large front porch with acres of groomed landscaping.

As they drove up to the house, he saw his mother and Etienne, his sister, sitting on a rocking swing on the front veranda. They were chatting while drinking glasses of wine and watching the sunset, which was something they did every evening after supper. They waved as the car approached the front entrance. A smile crossed Stephane's face. He was happy to be home so he could get back to work at the vineyard. This was where he felt most productive. His family meant everything to him, as they were a very close family.

The vehicle pulled up in front of the porch and stopped. His sister was the first to get up and run to him as he opened the car door and got out. She always embraced him when he came home from a long business trip, so he wasn't surprised when her arms opened wide to hug him.

"Welcome back! I missed you so much! How was your trip?" Etienne asked him as she kissed him on his cheek. His mother came down the steps right behind her.

"It went well. I missed you too," he answered, laughing and kissing her forehead. His younger sister was a petite woman with short brown hair, and she was bubbly all the time, but she was also very naïve in some aspects. Being ten years older than her, Stephane had always been Etienne's best friend and protector.

"Bonsoir, Maman," Stephane said as he stepped away from Etienne to give his mother a warm hug and a kiss.

"I'm glad you're back. Come; you must be tired. Are you hungry? I'll make you something to eat," his mother said as she took his hand to lead him inside, his sister in tow.

"No, I'm fine right now. Where's Papa?" Stephane asked as he walked into the house. He glanced into the library as he passed it, as that was where his father liked to sit in the evenings.

"He's in the production building checking out things, as usual," his mother answered him. He followed her into the kitchen and sat down on one of the stools at the counter. Etienne came and sat beside him.

He placed his hand on her knee and asked, "How's the engagement party coming along?" A smile brightened her face.

"I am so excited! The catering is all set, and the guest list will be going out on Friday. By the way, have you found a date for my social event yet? Or should I find one for you?" his sister teased as she lightly slapped his arm. His mind drifted back to Marcia, but he knew that was impossible considering she wouldn't give him the time of day.

"Don't worry about me. I still have a few weeks before the party, little sister. I'll find a date," he teased as he leaned forward and kissed her on the cheek.

She hugged him again, then said, "Well, if you don't find a date, I will. I know many girls that wouldn't mind going with you." Etienne giggled and walked away, leaving him alone with his mother, who was placing a tray of cheese, olives, and a few pieces of bread in front of him to eat.

"How are you doing? By the way, don't tell him I said this, but your father is working too hard. He has been so tired lately. Could you try to knock some sense into his thick head about slowing down?" his mother asked, concern filling her voice. She motioned with her hand for him to eat. "Eat!" Stephane reached over for a piece of cheese and popped it into his mouth. She always wanted to feed him.

"I'm good. I will take some of his duties now that I am back home, Maman," he answered as he chewed. He wondered if he would ever see Marcia again. *I must find a way to get her to go out with me. Why can't I stop thinking of her?* he thought.

"What's on your mind? You seem distant. Anything you want to talk about?" his mother asked him as she pulled a stool next to him and sat down. Stephane was quiet. He watched as she poured two glasses of wine and handed him one. He pondered if it was even worth mentioning Marcia considering she didn't seem to have any interest in him. Yet he couldn't stop thinking about her.

"No, Maman... Well, I met this girl. I like her, but she doesn't even know I exist, although I tried..." he mumbled, trailing off. He looked away from her, then grasped his glass of wine and took a drink.

"Oh! My dear son, don't give up that easily if you like her. I wouldn't give your father the time of day when I first met him, but, deep down, I couldn't get him out of my mind. Don't give up. She'll come around if it's meant to be." She laughed while rubbing his back with her hand, and then she grasped her glass and sipped her wine. He nodded at her, then reached over for another piece of cheese. She always knew how to comfort him.

* * *

Marcia woke up bright and early. When she glanced at the alarm clock, it was six o'clock. She showered quickly, then dressed in a summery, flower-printed dress. Standing in front of the mirror, she picked up her hairbrush and combed her hair. When she had worked as an escort, she had worn a lot of makeup in order to create a mask, causing her to now hate wearing too much of it. So today she chose to simply put on some lip gloss. She picked up her handbag and swung it over her shoulder. She locked her room, then headed downstairs, where the bus for her tour was waiting. Looking at her watch, she saw that she still had time for a cup of coffee and a baguette with jelly, which she grabbed from the concierge table in the lobby. Then, with long strides, she walked quickly toward the tour bus as she ate. She was so excited, she had butterflies in her stomach. She had wanted to visit a vineyard since she had arrived in France. It was one of her dreams. She sat down next to two older ladies, who appeared to be in their sixties. She rested her head back as soon as the bus started to progress down the road. Fifteen minutes later the bus was traveling on a route that was lined with row after row of green acres of grapes. It was the most beautiful sight Marcia had seen in a long time. *How beautiful! I'm so happy I came,* she thought.

She took her iPhone out of her pocket and snapped several pictures through the window. She could see the large vineyard estate in the background. She couldn't wait to visit the cellars and see the production aspect of winemaking—not to mention getting to tasting great champagne and wine. She sat at the edge of her seat during the rest of the drive, and the vehicle finally pulled in front of the main building and stopped. She directed her attention to the front of the bus, where the tour guide was giving instructions to the group.

"First, we will visit the cellars of the vineyards, where barrels of vintage champagne and wine are stored for over ten years before being sold to the stores. We will then make our way to the production area, where we can see how the grapes are separated and made into wine. And last—the best part—we will be tasting different champagnes in the lounge area, where we can also have a bite to eat. You can also purchase your favorite champagne or wine. If you are lucky, sometimes a member of the LaRoche family might come by and answer some of your questions. So, please stay with the group and do not wander. I will explain more as we progress into our tour," the guide instructed them, then turned and went down the stairs of the bus to wait for the group to disembark outside.

Marcia stood up immediately and began to make her way off the bus. She stood outside, where everyone was gathering by the entrance of one of the buildings. She relished in the adventure of learning new things. She noticed a beautiful house in the background, so she stepped to the side to take pictures of the villa. *I bet this home is at least a hundred years old. I wish I could see the inside; it must be grand*, she thought. Marcia followed the group closely. They first went downstairs to the cellars, where endless rows of oak barrels of champagne and bottles were stockpiled. She listened to their escort educate them about the wine as she took photos of the area. The group then ventured to the production section, where they learned about the process of harvesting the grapes—crushing, fermentation, clarification, and, finally, the aging of the wine. *Fascinating!* she thought. As she strolled along with the group, she looked up to the top floor and noticed a section of offices that had windows offering a view of the production area. She could see several people working at their desks, unaware of the group's presence. *They must be used to the tours*, she thought, continuing to follow the group.

Their next stop was the wine lounge, which had a shop where they could purchase a selection of wines and souvenirs. At the entrance of the room stood two young women, each holding a tray of flutes filled with champagne. She reached over and took a glass of wine, sipping it as she admired the inside of the store, which had prestigious awards hanging along the walls. The lounge still had the original wood beams on the ceiling as well as the original stonework on one of the walls, which must have dated from the nineteenth century, but everything else was very modern. She walked to one of the tables that was set up with a variety of cheeses and olives. She filled a small plate and nibbled on the snacks while reading framed magazine clippings about the various awards on the wall. She was hungry from the long tour. She finished her drink just as another one was offered to her by a waitress. Marcia thanked her, then drank another mouthful. The bubbles from the champagne were starting to make her feel lightheaded. She giggled quietly, hoping no one heard her or noticed. She didn't drink often, so the alcohol was starting to take its effect.

During all of the years she had been an escort, she had never drunk alcohol because she needed to be in control of any situation that could arise. She approached the food table again and picked up another tiny plate, which she filled with vegetables. She sat down in one of the chairs next to the table and crossed her legs. Most of the people were standing in front of her, mingling, so they were blocking her view of the front of the reception area. She was snacking quietly and savoring her drink when she heard a man's voice speaking at the other end of the room.

She stopped chewing immediately so she could listen. Her wine glass almost slipped from her grip. *I recognize that voice.* She tilted her head and leaned to the right, trying to see who was answering the questions from her group, but she couldn't see past them. *It can't be. I must be imagining it.* But how could she forget the sound of his voice? The man she had met in Paris. *What would he be doing here?* she asked herself, and then it hit her like a bolt of lightning. *Oh my God! No! No! No!* her mind screamed. This was LaRoche Vineyard. His last name was LaRoche...but it couldn't be. She hadn't matched it together when she had signed up for the excursion. Her hands began to shake.

Marcia placed her plate on the edge of the table. She swallowed her last bite, then slowly stood up. She peeked over the shoulder of the man who was in front of her. Her eyes widened, and her mouth popped open momentarily as her heart began to race. It was him. He was wearing a fitted, pinstriped gray suit and a matching tie. The color brought out his blue eyes, and the outfit showed off his physique. His hair was slicked back to perfection. There was nowhere to hide from him or escape him, because he was standing by the entrance. The sound of his tone invaded her. She studied him for several minutes as he answered the patron's questions. He was so smooth, knowledgeable, and professional. He was extremely handsome, and she was completely captivated by him. He stopped talking, and a wide smile appeared on his face. He was staring straight at her. *Oh God! I think he saw me. What am I going to do?*

She was sure that he had spotted her. Why else would he be looking in her direction and smiling? A few older folk turned to glance at her. She blushed on the spot, and she could feel heat rise to her ears. She raised her glass and took a sip of champagne, which didn't help, so she decided to ignore him. Marcia turned her back to him, pretending to examine the family crest on the wall, yet he was on her mind. She heard him say, "Enjoy your afternoon, everyone, and have more champagne. Now, if you'll excuse me." Footsteps approached her. *Stay calm*, she told herself.

Marcia couldn't move. She froze when she felt a gentle touch on her elbow. The mere contact of his skin on hers sent a warm feeling through her body. She closed her eyes for a moment and inhaled deeply.

"Bonjour, Marcia. It's nice to see you again," he said from behind her. She spun around slowly and looked up at him. The grin on his face made her think that he must have seen her flush earlier. She lifted her chin and stood up straight.

"Good morning. What are you doing here?" she asked, trying to avoid his blue eyes. He was standing so close that she could smell his musk fragrance. She took a slight step back so she could gain control of herself, but her heartbeat still continued to accelerate.

"This vineyard belongs to my family. What are you doing in Epernay?" he questioned, still not taking his eyes off of her. This time she didn't brush him away like she had done all the other times they had met.

"I just came to spend some time in Epernay and visit a few vineyards," she explained as she saw the group move toward the exit.

"That's great! Why don't you let me show you around town while you're here? How long are you going to be staying? I'm so happy to be able to see you again," he said to her. Again, he never took his eyes off of her as he stood in front of her. It was as if there was no one else around but her.

"I don't know...my group is leaving. I think I have to get going; otherwise the bus will leave and..." She trailed off as she pointed toward the entrance. He turned to look at them, then quickly turned back to her. She wanted to move, but he was blocking her path, and it was as if her feet were planted on the floor.

"Please, don't go just yet. Stay! Have lunch with me. I promise to be a complete gentleman. After our dinner I'll drive you back to anywhere you say. I swear," he begged, then raised his hand up as if he were swearing it to her.

It made her smile. She looked down at her feet for a second, unable to agree, unsure if she should go or not. She had told herself she wouldn't get involved with any man for a while, and now she was in this situation. She *did* like him a lot. He was persistent, and she wanted to spend more time with him. After all, this was their third meeting, and he hadn't given up yet. She glanced at him, then nodded.

"All right. Just lunch, and then you'll drive me back to my hotel in town, agreed?" she whispered. He nodded, and she could see that his eyes were dancing with joy. He smiled; it made her melt when it reappeared on his face. He seemed so excited that she had said yes.

"Perfect! I need to go to the main house, change my clothes, and..." he stopped talking. He reached for her hand, and his touch made her whole body tingle. She pulled her hand away. He took a step closer, only inches away from her, then looked down at her. She could feel his body heat. He licked his lips. His face was so close to hers that she could feel his breath on her face. *He's going to kiss me,* she thought, but then he pulled away.

"Don't disappear on me again, okay," he whispered.

"I won't. What house?" she asked, although she knew very well what he meant. But she just wanted to make sure she was right and to continue making conversation.

"This vineyard belongs to my family; our home is right next door," he answered, a wince on his face. Then he pointed in the direction of the villa. He extended his right hand to her. She glanced at it but didn't take it.

"Okay, but I have to let the tour guide know I'm not going back with them," she responded. He offered his hand again. This time she let him take it. It fit perfectly in his, and he gently squeezed hers.

"Come on. I'm taking you with me to the house. I don't want you to change your mind and leave while I'm changing my clothes. I need some more casual attire," he answered. They started walking toward the exit of the lounge. He stopped a young woman on the way to tell her to go inform the tour guide that Marcia wasn't going back on the bus, and then Stephane thanked her. Neither of them said a word as they left the lounge. As a result of all of the alcohol she had drank, Marcia couldn't stop giggling. She held his hand tightly as they walked down the stone pathway and headed toward the villa. She felt like a teenager on her first date.

Chapter 5

Stephane had not been able to believe his eyes when he had looked across the room at the crowd of tourists while answering questions about the vineyard. There she had been, wearing a flowered dress, the most gorgeous sight he had ever seen. All of his thoughts about losing her had disappeared when he spotted her, and his heart had healed. He had been given a new chance at love, and this time he was not going to fail. His emotions had been racing. He couldn't focus on anything but her. He had quickly finished the Q&A session so he could make his way to her. Her back had been turned to him, and he had slowed his pace as he approached her. He had known that he needed to make sure he had the right words prepared to convince her to go out with him. His hand had trembled when he stretched out his fingers to touch her. When she had pivoted around to face him, he had known she was the one that he wanted to spend time with.

Now they were sauntering down the cobblestone path, on their way to the villa so he could change and take her to lunch. *I should have kissed her when I had the chance. I just wanted to taste her lips, but then she might have run away again*, he thought. Not a word was said between them while they walked hand in hand until they were halfway to the front door. He kept peeking her way to make sure she was real. Her blond hair was bouncing in the wind with every step she took. *The best part is that she didn't pull her hand away from me. That must be a good sign. Her giggles are sweet; it must be the champagne*, he thought.

"I saw the villa on my way here. It's absolutely stunning. How old is it?" she asked him. He noticed that she never looked his way, instead keeping her sight on the house.

"My grandfather built it in the early 1900s. My father was born here, as were his two brothers, but they weren't interested in the wine industry. My father was captivated by the wine business, and he loves to drink wine too," he joked. She laughed.

"And what about you?" she asked.

"Oh! I love all aspects of the company, and I like to drink wine too...but in moderation." He chuckled as they arrived at the front porch.

"Here we are. If you want, you can have a seat on the swing. I'll hurry and be right back," he told her as he pointed to the seat that was hanging from the ceiling. They walked up the three steps, and he brought her to the swing. He knew he had to let go of her hand. They stood so close, and when he saw her full lips part slightly, he wanted to wrap his arms around her waist, pull her near his body, and kiss her. He took a step back again and reluctantly let go of her hand. She moved forward and sat down on the seat without a word.

"I'll be right back. Don't go anywhere. Five minutes, okay?" he told her. She looked at him and nodded. He swung the front door open, then strode through the foyer and took the staircase two steps at a time as he went up to his bedroom. He had his jacket and tie off before he even entered his closet. He finished undressing quickly, letting the clothes fall where they may. He just wanted to get back to Marcia as quickly as he could. He was so afraid that she might not be there when he returned. He grabbed a pair of Burberry jeans and a white Hugo Boss linen shirt, then threw everything on. He buttoned the shirt as he slipped a pair of loafers on. After stopping in front of his dresser and spraying on a touch of cologne, he hurried back downstairs.

He slowed his pace when he got to the bottom of the stairs so he could catch his breath. He noticed someone sitting with her: his sister, Etienne. He walked outside as casually as he could, trying not to let them know how nervous he was. He took a deep breath before he went outside, and then he spoke.

"I'm back! I see you met my sister," he said as he gave Marcia a smile. Etienne stood up when she heard her brother speak.

"Yes, we met. It was a pleasure to meet you, Marcia. Have a great lunch, and I hope to see you again," Etienne told Marcia. She walked over to her brother, kissed his cheek, and then whispered in his ear, "She's very nice. Keep her!"

"Thank you! It was lovely meeting you too," Marcia responded, not moving from her spot, her eyes on Stephane. Etienne quickly disappeared through the front door of the villa.

"Are you ready?" Stephane asked Marcia, a bit uneasy. He was hoping Marcia hadn't heard his sister's words, but he brushed it off. He offered his hand to her, which she took immediately. He was pleased that she hadn't rebuffed him.

"What do you feel like eating?" he inquired as they walked around the house, heading to where his Bentley was parked. He reached over and opened the car door, and she slipped into the seat without a word. He went to sit into the driver's seat, then turned his head to peek at her. She was putting her seatbelt on, so he did the same. He noticed the car didn't seem to impress her, as she never asked any questions about it, nor did she comment on it. She crossed her legs, then pulled her hem above her knee, exposing her long tanned legs. He was getting aroused just looking at her, and his fingers gripped the steering wheel tightly. He saw her place both of her hands on her knee before looking straight ahead. *Keep your mind straight or you might lose her*, he thought.

"You don't speak much, do you? Anything you feel like eating? Or should I ask how hungry you are?" he questioned before starting the engine and shifting it into drive.

She grinned at him, then answered, "Right now I'd eat a horse! I'm famished." They both laughed out loud, and it seemed to break the ice between them. He looked at her and smiled. He couldn't stop glancing her way as he drove toward town. He was a happy man when sitting next to Marcia. He couldn't wait to know everything about her.

A half hour later he guided his car into the parking lot of Brasserie Le Central—a quaint restaurant on Place de la Republique that was famous not only for its wines but also for its ales. The food consisted of authentic local dishes. He hoped she would enjoy it.

"Here we are. Would you like to sit inside or on the terrace?" Stephane asked as he stepped out of the car and walked around to open her door. Marcia swung her legs out gracefully, then stood up next to him. He closed the car door behind her. He raised his arm and offered it to her. She tilted her head, grinned at him, and then, to his delight, slipped her arm through his. There was nothing he liked more than her touch against him.

"Let's sit inside...that is, if you don't mind," she answered as they sauntered toward the entrance of the establishment. They stepped through the opened entryway and were greeted by Jean-Pierre, the owner, who was standing at a small podium near the bar.

"Bonjour, Stephane, how are you?" he asked as he grabbed two menus from the pile next to him.

"Bonjour, Jean-Pierre. I'm very good, thank you," Stephane answered as he looked over his shoulder toward the back of the restaurant.

"Your usual table?" Jean-Pierre asked casually, and then, not waiting for Stephane's answer, he took a step forward in the direction of the back.

"Yes, thank you. After you, Marcia," Stephane said as he gently placed his hand on the lower part of her back, urging her forward. They followed Jean-Pierre past the numerous red leather booths and tables that were draped with gold tablecloths, then stopped at the booth that had a large window overlooking the street. Marcia glided into the seat, and Stephane took the one across from her, but in reality, he wanted to sit next to her.

Jean-Pierre placed their menus on the table and said, "I'll send your waiter over. Enjoy!"

"Thank you, Jean-Pierre," Stephane answered him, then looked up at Marcia. She had her hands folded on her menu, and her head was turned toward the window. She was observing the people who were walking by. She looked beautiful as the rays of the sunshine shined against her face. He noticed she wasn't wearing any makeup, and he liked the natural look. Most women he met wore too much. He reached over and placed his hand over hers. His touch seemed to bring her back to life, and she slowing pulled her hands back and picked up her menu.

"This is a wonderful spot to sit at. You can almost see the whole street. You come here often, don't you?" she asked as she cast her eyes down to look at her menu.

"Yes, I do. Jean-Pierre and I have known each other since we were in grade school. Everyone knows each other in this town," he told her. She kept her eyes on the list of selections.

"Would you like a drink? Wine or ale?" he asked as he saw the server headed their way. She glanced up at him.

"I think I've had enough wine for today, but I'll have a Pelforth and the lasagna a la bolognaise. I love dark beer. What about you?" she answered confidently as she closed the menu.

"Wow! I love a woman who knows what she wants. I'll have the same," he answered. The waiter came by the table. He placed an assortment of breads and croissants in front of them, and then Stephane gave him their order. The waiter left them alone so he could put in their orders. Marcia's attention was once again on the people walking by the window. Stephane reached over and tenderly placed his right hand over hers.

"So, tell me what brought you to France? And how long do you plan on staying?" he inquired, hoping she would be staying for a while so he would have time to get to know her better. She redirected her attention back to him as soon as he touched her.

"I'm sorry, what did you say?" she asked him, seemingly preoccupied with her thoughts. The good part was that she didn't break away from his touch this time.

"I asked what brought you to France? Are you here vacationing, or are you here for work?" he repeated. He stared at every aspect of her face—her dark eyes, her high cheekbones, and her full lips. She frowned at him for an instant, seeming to be unsure of how to answer, but then she smiled at him.

"Well, I've always wanted to live in Paris, so I decided to take a year off after my studies, and I moved here to explore the countryside and figure out what I want to do in the future," she answered him, and then she pulled her hands away from his and placed them on her lap. His heart skipped a beat at the joy he felt from knowing that she would be around for a year and that he might have a chance to get to know her better. She hadn't said much on the ride over to the restaurant, but now he had hope and a goal to make her his.

"Oh! That's adventurous. It would be my pleasure if you would let me show you a few places around town or in Paris," he told her. She lifted her head and looked at him for a minute without saying a single word, and it seemed like an eternity. The sheer silence was killing him. He waited patiently as she appeared to be trying to make her decision on what to say. His eyes met hers, and he held his breath in anticipation, worrying that she would refuse him. He watched her as she bit her lower lip and sat up straight in her seat. She seemed to be thinking about her answer, and then she gave him a smile.

"Yes, that would be nice. I don't know too many people around here," she said calmly, not moving a muscle. He closed his eyes for a second, trying to regroup his senses. Had she finally accepted his proposal? Yes, she had agreed, and he was elated and completely filled with desire.

"Perfect! I would love to take you around and show you all the sights," he answered, excited at the prospect of spending more time with her. He would savor every moment she gave him. The server arrived with their drinks and placed the ales in front of them, then left them alone. Stephane grasped his glass and lifted his drink to make a toast.

"To a new beginning and...the sights of Epernay and Paris," he said. She picked up her glass and nodded at him, then took a sip of her ale.

* * *

Marcia sat in the booth and looked at him, unsure of how to answer this man that she had been trying to avoid getting involved with since coming to Paris. It seemed as if their paths kept crossing. It had to mean something. He wanted to spend time with her. She was used to being paid to entertain men, with no emotions involved. That was her job: to never get attached to her clients. It was always business; she faked every feeling for them and shielded her heart from them. Now, here she was staring at Stephane. He was clueless about her former profession, and she was living in a different country. She was free of her past, and she would never have to tell him. He seemed nervous, and she watched him rake his fingers through his hair. *Isn't this what you always wanted...to meet a man who cares for you?* she pondered. *But will you be able to keep your past a secret. What if he ever found out? You would be heartbroken. But he's right in front of you, and he has pursued you since you boarded that plane to come here. And you haven't forgotten him.* She had never felt this way about a man until now. There was a sexual attraction between them, and she had an overwhelming desire to want to know everything about him. She had to chance it, so she decided to take the plunge.

The smile that appeared on his face after she accepted his offer sent goosebumps of lust down her spine. She had forgotten how it felt to be wanted by a man who didn't pay for her services. During the next hour she felt relaxed as they ate their food and drank more ale. She laughed at his jokes and chatted about the town. She never divulged much about herself, instead learning about him. She was being cautious about giving out her personal information now. She needed to trust him, and then maybe she would tell him more about her life.

"How about we go for a walk down General LeClerc Street? It's right around the corner. I know this great place called Patisserie Vincent Dallet. It's famous for its chocolate desserts," he mentioned, then pointed at the place through the window. He folded his napkin and placed it on the top of the table.

She did the same and answered, "Sure, I'd like that."

He took out a hundred euro note from his pocket and dropped it on the table next to the bill. She slipped out of her seat and started walking toward the exit of the restaurant. Stephane followed closely behind. She hadn't taken three strides on the sidewalk when she felt his hand wrap around hers. He squeezed it and kept walking down the street. Marcia didn't object. She felt a sense of belonging after noticing that most of the Frenchmen held the hands of their mates. They strolled down the street slowly as she admired the architecture of the buildings.

"Do you see the line of patrons waiting to be served up ahead? That's where we are going. His patisseries are so delicious. People wait in line for a table, but if you prefer, we can take it to go. We can find a bench somewhere so we can sit and eat?" he told her as they approached the patisserie.

"Why don't we take it to go? I'd rather stay outside since it's such a beautiful day," she responded as they stood in line at the entrance of the store. He let go of her hand, but a second later she felt it on the lower part of her back. She could feel him rubbing gently up and down her spine. She pretended not to be aware of his touch, yet every stroke made her hungry for more of his caresses. He was quiet until they stepped into the boutique, which was filled with counters of succulent pastries waiting to be tasted. There were small gateaux, éclairs, and macaroons. Unbelievable designs of every shape and color were all behind a large glass, serving as temptation for the customers. She bent down a bit at the glass and examined all of the different choices.

"What would you like?" Marcia heard Stephane ask as she was trying to make her selection. She looked up at him and shrugged her shoulders.

"Oh my God! Everything looks so scrumptious. I can't decide. You pick," she told him. She felt like a child in a candy store.

"Bonjour, we will have a dozen assorted pastries," he told the young lady behind the counter, who grabbed a box and started putting the desserts in.

"I hope you have room for all of those." Marcia laughed, surprised that he had asked for so many. She followed him to the end of the counter as he paid for the desserts. He picked up the box in one hand and grabbed her hand with the other.

"Come on. Let's find a place to sit," he told her as he led her outside of the pastry shop. He turned to his right, dragging her playfully down the block. There was a small square with yellow and red flowers, and tall trees surrounded the perimeter of the garden. There was a row of benches against the far end of the park.

"Hmmm! You really know the area, don't you?" she said, laughing as she sat down next to him on one of the cement seats. He placed the box on top of her knees and opened it.

"Yes, I do know the area. I've lived in this town my whole life. My parents used to bring us here every Sunday afternoon for a treat when I was a child. I still love to come here and watch people while I dig into these gateaux. You get the first choice." Stephane said as he pointed for her to choose one of the desserts.

"Too many options," she answered as she licked her lips, never taking her eyes off of the goods. She rarely indulged in delicacies, as she was afraid she might get addicted to the sweets and gain weight.

"I'll tell you what. You can have a bite of all of them, and I'll have the leftovers," he teased her. She shot him a quick look and snickered at him.

"Okay, let's start with this one," Marcia said, and then she singled out the mini chocolate cake, picking it up with her thumb and index finger. She brought the pastry to her mouth and took a tiny bite. It was very tasty as it melted in her mouth. She glanced up at him. He had a silly grin on his face. He reached over, took her hand, and brought her fingers to his mouth. The wet sensation of his lips against her fingers made her pause, heat building between her legs. She wanted more, and she watched as his eyes never left hers. He raised his hand so it touched her cheek, and she didn't move. She wondered what might happen as his face neared hers. She closed her eyes and waited. She had never wanted to kiss a man as much as she wanted to kiss him.

"You have a little frosting on your lip," he whispered to her. Suddenly her eyes flew open. His thumb came down on the corner of her mouth to wipe the frosting off. She turned her face away as heat rose to her ears, embarrassed at the thought of her desires.

Chapter 6

Stephane yearned to press his lips against hers, but at the last minute, he pulled away because he was afraid she might rebuff his advances and be offended by his proposition. So he simply wiped the frosting from her face. It had taken so long for her to talk to him and spend time with him. He couldn't risk losing her.

"So, did you want another one, or are you going to let me choose this time?" he asked as casually as he could without letting her know how nervous he was. She looked at him silently, then lifted the box up from her knees and placed it on his.

"Your turn to choose, but be warned that I prefer the strawberry tart," she said. She gave him the biggest smile, and at that moment, he knew she was the right woman for him.

They sat on the bench for another hour as they learned about each other's pasts and goals. He loved hearing her laugh and watching as the wind blew her hair away from her face, exposing her long, thin neck that he longed to kiss. He loved how she always bit her lower lip every time she tried to think of an answer to one of his questions. They walked back to his car hand in hand, and then he drove her to her hotel. He ran around the car and opened her door. She gracefully stepped out, both legs at one time, and stood so close to him that he could smell her perfume. He didn't want her to leave, and he couldn't wait to see her again.

"Let me ask you a question. Did you enjoy your day with me?" he asked her.

"Yes, thank you very much for everything," she answered shyly.

"I had a great time. So, tell me, can I persuade you to go out to dinner tomorrow night?" he asked, and then he held his breath, hoping she wouldn't refuse him.

She raised her hand and stroked his arm lightly, never looking at him, and then she walked away from him. She took three long steps, then turned, peeked at him over her shoulder, smiled, and yelled, "I'll be ready at seven. Don't be late. I'll be waiting."

He continued to observe her as joy invaded him. She held her head high, and her hips rocked from left to right under her flowing dress as she walked away. She never looked back as she disappeared through the front door of the hotel.

Stephane stood immobile, his hands in his pockets, wishing he could go inside with her. His mind drifted to how she would have tasted if he had kissed her in the park. *I should have kissed her.* He returned and sat in the driver's seat, a grin on his face. He would see her again tomorrow. He drove home in silence as his thoughts wandered to Marcia and where he would take her the following evening. He needed to take her somewhere special—somewhere where he could be alone with her on his date. However, he was limited on options in Epernay. The town was small, and there weren't many places to take her. He would have to think about that one.

A few minutes later he was back at the vineyard. He parked his Bentley in the courtyard and noticed a sports car parked near the entrance. It belonged to Mason, Etienne's fiancée. He entered the villa two steps at a time. He could smell the aroma of his mother's cooking as soon as he marched inside. *She sure loves to cook and entertain,* he thought, *especially when she has someone that enjoys eating her food.* He chuckled, then shook his head.

"Stephane, where did you disappear to this afternoon? I called your cell phone, but you never answered. It must be that girl I met today. You should bring her over more often. I liked her," Etienne said, then winked at him. She poured him a glass of wine from the bottle sitting on kitchen counter and passed it to him. He saw that Mason was having a conversation with his and Etienne's father in the living room area.

"I was...um...busy," Stephane told her as he took a sip from his drink. He heard his sister giggle. He didn't want to jinx his luck and tell her too much about Marcia just yet. Etienne vanished as she joined her fiancée in the other room. Stephane strolled over to his mother, who was checking the vegetables on the stove. He kissed his mother on the cheek.

"Bonsoir, Maman," he said to her as he tried to see what she was making for supper. He put his hand out, but she slapped it lightly, just as she used to do when he was a child and she wanted him to leave the kitchen.

"Get out and go join Mason and your father," she teased him. He laughed out loud and took a step back. He wasn't hungry; all he had on his mind was Marcia. He just liked to pick on his mother.

"Supper is almost ready. Why don't you go say hi to Mason?" his mother suggested to him, then continued to prepare her meal by stirring what looked like a hollandaise sauce.

"Okay, okay," he answered. Stephane walked away and went to greet his future brother-in-law. Etienne had met him the previous year at an international wine seminar in Monaco. She instantly fell in love with him. He was a CEO of a construction company from the New York City area. In Stephane's eyes, he was a charmer and a drunk, but Stephane wouldn't say anything to his sister to hurt her. Mason flew to Paris every other weekend so he could spend time with Etienne.

"How are you? I was hoping to see you when I arrived earlier today," Mason said to Stephane when he saw him enter the room. He extended his hand and shook Stephane's. Stephane could smell alcohol on his breath.

"Sorry I'm late. I was in town taking care of some business," Stephane lied. He didn't want them to know about Marcia just yet. He sat down across from them on one of the chairs near the marble fireplace.

"How about a round of golf tomorrow at Reims Champagne? Tee time is nine o'clock. A few of my friends are joining me. We could have a couple of drinks afterward," Mason said to Stephane. Stephane hated to decline his offer, but he didn't have time to go golfing, and he didn't like Mason's American friends anyway. He had missed most of the workday because he went out with Marcia, and he had to catch up on his paperwork, but he had no regrets. Most of all, he needed to find a special place to take Marcia to the next day. A vision of her appeared in his mind, and he pursed his lips while thinking of her. He was brought back to reality when he heard Mason say, "That difficult of a decision, Stephane?" Laughter followed his comment. He looked up at Mason and grinned.

"I think I will pass on golf tomorrow. I have too much work to catch up on. Maybe next time," he answered, taking a sip from his drink.

"All right. I'll make sure to get a rain check. I'm going to be here through the next two week anyway...until our engagement party," he told Stephane.

Stephane observed as Etienne came back from the kitchen and snuggled next to Mason on the couch.

"Maman just said dinner that is ready and for us to come sit down in the dining room," Etienne announced as she took Mason by the hand to escort him.

"Great! I'm famished," Mason told her, and he stood up. Stephane noticed that Mason seemed a little unsteady on his feet as he proceeded toward the dining area. Stephane gulped the last drops of his wine, then trailed behind them, all the while daydreaming of a perfect afternoon to spend with Marcia.

The next morning Stephane dressed in black Valentino pants and a blue Hugo Boss button down shirt. He sat behind the desk in his office and gazed through the large window at the green fields of grapes in the backyard of the vineyard. His mind was preoccupied, and he couldn't focus on his work. His feet rested on the corner of his desk as he leaned back in his chair. His right hand tapped his pen against the edge of his mahogany desk as his other hand rested on his cheek while he contemplated where he could take Marcia for dinner. He wanted to take her somewhere where they could be alone. He had never had a problem before when deciding where to take a woman, but he was feeling nervous about this date.

"Hey! Where did you take off to so early this morning? You rarely miss breakfast," his sister asked as she walked into his office and flopped down in the leather chair across from his desk.

"Oh! I wasn't too hungry. I just grabbed a cup of coffee and came back here to work," he answered as he took his feet down, pivoted his chair so he was facing her, and smiled.

"Hmm, that's unusual. What's wrong? I know you too well. What are you hiding behind those blue eyes of yours? It must be a girl!" Etienne questioned him with a suppressed laugh, not taking her eyes off of him. Stephane shifted his weight in his seat, glanced to his left to avoid her stare, and then smirked as he thought of Marcia. He didn't want to say anything about her just yet, but he couldn't lie to his sister. They were too close, and she would know he fibbed.

"I'm trying to decide where to take my date for dinner this evening. I want it to be special. I like this girl," he quietly said to her. Then he took a deep breath while he waited for the laughter to come roaring from his sister.

"Oh my God!" She paused, then snickered again.

"Since when does my brother have a problem..." she said, then stopped mid-sentence as her mouth opened and she smiled at him. Stephane tilted his head at her, trying to be as casual as possible, not giving anything away. She scooted her butt to the edge of her seat and leaned her elbow against the desk to examine him. He swiveled his chair around so it was facing the window, without a word. Stephane didn't want his sister to see his face, because she would ask too many questions that he either didn't want to or couldn't answer about Marcia.

"It's not a problem. I'll figure it out," Stephane lied, hoping she would go away, but he knew her too well. He cringed when he heard her burst out laughing, then braced himself for the interrogation.

"Oh no, you don't. Who is she? Tell me. It's the woman who was on the swing yesterday, isn't it?" his sister asked, and then he heard her get up from her chair. She took two steps around his desk and came to stand in front of him, her arms folded in front of her. He laughed nervously as he looked up at her.

"She's just a girl I met...that's all," Stephane told her as he tried to rotate his chair around again, but she put her hand on the back of his chair to stop him from turning.

"What's her name? Where is she from? What does she do for work? You like her, don't you? You never shy away from talking to me about your women," Etienne said, then leaned against his desk. She wasn't going away, and he knew that, so he figured that he might as well tell her a little bit about Marcia.

"All right, her name is Marcia Philips. I met her a few weeks ago in Paris, when I came back from America, and she's in Epernay for a couple of days. Yes, I like her. I have been trying to figure out a special place to take her for dinner, but it needs to be somewhere other than a restaurant. That's all! Now go away so I can think," he informed her playfully. He picked up a contract from the top of his desk and pretended to read it. He noticed that she still hadn't moved from her spot, so he glanced up at her. She had her index finger on her lips, and her eyes were looking up at the ceiling as if she was thinking.

"I know where you can take her. It's very romantic, but it might cost you a pretty penny," she told him, jumping up.

"I don't care about the money. Where? Tell me!" he said to her, immediately interested in her response. He put the papers down on his desk, looked up at her, and waited for her to answer.

"There's a company called Champagne by Balloons. You can hire them. It's right here in Epernay. They take you on a balloon ride that overlooks the Reims. It's romantic. You could bring a picnic basket with you so you can have dinner when you land, and Andre could pick you up afterward. There you go: beautiful evening!" Etienne told him excitedly. She lifted her hand up for a high five. He wasn't sure if it was a good idea, but it was original. He would be alone with Marcia, except for the operator of the balloon, and she might enjoy it. He slowly lifted his hand up and slapped hers lightly.

"Okay, I'll check into it. Now go away so I can work," he ordered again as he pointed toward the door.

"It's really idyllic. I did it a few years ago with friends, and it was fun. I'll tell Maman to make you a gourmet basket. She will be pleased you like a girl," she announced before starting to walk away from his office.

"Etienne!" he called out to her. He watched as she turned around to face him.

"Please, let's keep this between us and not tell Maman anything. She will ask too many questions, I'm not prepared to answer any just yet, okay?" he pleaded with her. She wrinkled her nose in disapproval but nodded her head in agreement.

"Very well, I will pretend the basket is for me and Mason, but you'll have to give me the details. She *will* find out eventually," she joked, then strolled away from the office. Stephane sat motionless, thinking. It was a splendid idea. He immediately looked it up on his computer and then picked up his phone so he could make the arrangements for that evening.

* * *

Marcia leaned her head back against the rim of the tub, closing her eyes as she soaked her body in lavender oils and prepared for her date with Stephane. Soft, romantic music by Adele played in the background of her room. She had never imagined she would come to a foreign country and meet a man that she was interested in. Stephane had been the furthest thing from her mind when she had boarded that plane weeks ago. But she hadn't been able to help herself. It seemed as if she had been drawn to him as soon as she had seen him. What were the chances they would meet again? It was fate, but she didn't want to get her hopes up and then have them shattered the following week. She couldn't concentrate on anything but him all day. "I wonder where he'll take me. Will he kiss me? Will he ask me out again?" she asked out loud as she relaxed in the warm water.

A half hour later she decided she would not overdress. She picked out a black pair of jeans and a red, silk blouse from the closet. She placed them on her bed. *That should do*, she thought. She settled with a pair of flat shoes since she was in the country and hadn't brought much with her—she hadn't planned on dating anyone special.

She dressed and then stood in front of the mirror as she tried to decide if she should leave her hair down or put it up. She finally twirled her hair up and made a messy bun. She looked at the clock on her night table. It was almost seven o'clock. She picked up her keys and her shoulder bag, then hurried out of the door, going down the stairs and into the lobby. She opened the front door of the villa and stepped outside to see if Stephane had arrived. She hadn't told him where she would meet him, so she doubted he would be there. However, to her surprise he was there waiting for her. She instantly smiled when she saw him. He was leaning against the front of his blue Bentley, his arms folded across his chest and his feet crossed nonchalantly. Flowers were resting on the hood next to him. She glanced past him and saw someone who appeared to be his chauffeur sitting behind the wheel.

Impressive! she thought. He looked handsome and distinguished in his outfit of all black. When he saw her, he straightened up and began walking toward her. She didn't move from her spot as she watched him approach her one step at a time, his gaze never leaving hers. He was holding a bouquet of at least two dozen red roses in one hand.

"Bonsoir, beautiful! How are you?" he asked when he was a few feet away. She was used to getting compliments from her clients, but they never meant anything to her. However, compliments coming from Stephane made her ears burn. She smirked at him.

"Bonsoir, Monsieur. I am well, and I must say, you don't look so bad yourself." She giggled at him. He smiled at her and then, to her surprise, came forward and kissed her on the cheek. His lips were so soft, and she wanted more.

"These are for you," he said, placing the roses in her arms.

"Thank you so much. You didn't have to do that. They are gorgeous," Marcia said. She brought them to her nose and inhaled the fragrance. They walked side by side to the Bentley. She watched as the chauffeur opened the back door, and Stephane motioned with his hand for her to have a seat.

"After you," he said, so she moved past him and took a seat in the back seat. Seconds later he sat beside her and closed the door. As soon as they were both seated, his chauffeur started the car and rolled away from the hotel. She placed the roses on her knees and looked down at them. She loved red roses; they were her favorite flowers. The whole car smelled of its fragrance. He reached over and took them from her.

"Let me put them on the front seat. It will give you more room," he told her. She observed him as he delicately dropped them next to the chauffeur, but when he glided back in the seat, he slid closer to her. His knee touched hers. He didn't pull it away, and she didn't move; she liked the feeling. He lifted his right arm and placed it behind her on the seat. Marcia still didn't move an inch. She felt lust invade her—a warm, comfortable feeling. It was as if he belonged next to her. Stephane was so close to her that she could smell his aftershave, and it drove her wild.

"So where are you taking me?" Marcia asked, trying to distract herself from his touch.

"Well, are you afraid of heights? That's your only clue," Stephane said, and then he turned to face her. He was inches from her lips. The temptation to kiss him was almost insurmountable. She licked her lips slowly, then turned her head away from him and pretended to look at the scenery.

"Not really. Why?" she asked quietly as she tried to refrain from turning toward him and kissing him. She needed to gain her composure. She was sure he could hear her heart beating through her chest. She could barely breathe. She had never felt this way with her emotions with any of the men she had been with. She was always in control. She always knew what to say, how to act, she was never shy, but they were also paying for her services. She couldn't think straight. This was all new to her.

"I'm taking you somewhere special. I'm not going to tell you where. You will just have to be patient and wait," he told her.

She felt his hand on her shoulder, and he rubbed her exposed neck with one of his fingers. A sexual feeling went all the way down between her legs. She still didn't budge as she enjoyed his touch.

"Very well, then. Do you always treat your women this way, not telling them where you are taking them?" she asked him.

"Only the special ones I truly like," he replied. She giggled. They drove down the countryside for about a half hour admiring the long fields of green slopes. They finally turned down a dirt road, and she saw it. It took her breath away. Her hand went up to her mouth in disbelief.

"Oh my God! I can't believe it. That's why you asked me if I was afraid of heights?" she asked as she pushed herself forward in her seat for a better view. Up ahead she could see a hot air balloon in a field, with a man standing beside it. It had red, yellow, and orange stripes.

"Yes, I thought you might want to see the region from up above. I'm pleased you like it," he said, smiling at her.

"I absolutely cannot wait. I'm so excited," she answered him. She bounced up and down in her seat like a child. She couldn't take her eyes off the balloon as the chauffeur pulled up beside it. She was so thrilled she kept jumping up and down. She kept glancing at him then back to the balloon. She heard him laugh. She felt his hand on her lower back. She wanted to turn and kiss him, but she resisted. It was something she had always wanted to do, yet she had never had the opportunity to do. Stephane took her hand and opened his door. She slid down the seat and followed him, not resisting his touch. She walked beside him in silence.

They couldn't walk fast enough for her. She wanted to run up to the balloon. The chauffeur casually walked up to the balloon and placed the picnic basket inside.

"Bonsoir, Mr. LaRoche, Mademoiselle. My name is Julian. I will be your guide and the operator of our fabulous Champagne balloon," the man said when they were near, extending his hand to shake Stephane's hand, then Marcia's. Marcia quietly stood beside her date, looking up at the balloon in awe.

"Please, call me Stephane, and this is Marcia," Stephane said as he introduced her. Marcia momentarily greeted the man.

"Nice to meet you," she managed to say.

"I am ready to depart whenever you are. I'll give you the information and instructions on how this works while we are in the air. You just need to hop in," he told them.

"Ready?" Stephane looked Marcia's way, and she nodded immediately, smiling from ear to ear. She looked at the wicker basket, which was about four feet in height, and took a step toward it. She was trying to figure out how to gracefully get in when she heard Stephane say, "Let me help you." Then she felt his arms around her body. He scooped her up and held her tight against his chest. She wrapped her arms around his neck without protest, and he carried her to the gondola, gently dropping her inside. Seconds later he jumped in beside her.

They watched and listened in silence as Julian instructed his partner on the ground to untie the ropes, and then Julian started to pilot the balloon.

"By using the burners to heat the inside of the envelope of the balloon, I can control the altitude," Julian explained. Flames shot up, and the balloon filled with warm air and lifted off of the ground. Marcia gripped the rim of the basket with both hands. She held her breath as excitement invaded her soul. She looked down at the ground; they were ten, or maybe even twenty, feet high, and they kept climbing up. She had always wanted to experience a balloon ride, but she had never had the chance.

Suddenly she felt a strong arm wrap around her waist as Stephane pulled her near his body. She didn't resist; instead she enjoyed the warmth of his body against hers. She turned her head slightly to face him, and Stephane whispered into her ear, "Are you enjoying your surprise? Are you okay? Afraid?"

"No, I'm not scared now that you are near me. This is unbelievable," Marcia answered him. She felt him tighten his grasp around her, and his whole body rubbed against her back. They lifted to almost one thousand meters, which provided panoramic landscape views of the valleys and hillsides of Reims. They stood glued together for most of the flight as they admired the scenery. It was magical. His head was cuddled against her shoulder, and Marcia could feel his warm breath against her naked neck. She was happy. For the first time in a long time, she felt wanted and liked where she was. She could be herself with him.

Marcia heard the pop of a champagne bottle behind her. She looked in the direction of the noise and saw that Julian had opened a bottle of LaRoche Champagne. He was pouring two flutes of the bubbly. Stephane took a step back so he could take the glasses from Julian, then passed one to her. She felt a cool breeze on her back when he moved away, but he was back beside her within seconds. He lifted his glass up to hers as he peered into her eyes. She wanted him, and a hot sensation invaded her body all the way down to her core. He was so good-looking, especially when she gazed into those blue eyes.

"Marcia," he said, "I am so content that you finally agreed to come on a date with me. May we have many more evenings like tonight."

"Yes, that would be nice," was all that her lips uttered. He touched his glass to hers, and they both took a mouthful of champagne before setting the flutes on a table nearby. Marcia knew that what happened afterward would be engraved in her memory forever. He came forward, seized her by the waistline, and brought her close to his hard body. He raised his hands and cupped her face. She didn't protest as his lips parted and his mouth came forward to meet hers. She wrapped her arms around his waist. He tasted like champagne, and his tongue moved slowly in rhythm with hers as a cold breeze pushed her hair backwards. She closed her eyes as sexual urges that had been dormant for years resurfaced. She didn't want it to end, but she needed to catch her breath. Their mouths separated as she pulled away, and her lips were tingling. They were both breathing hard. He let go and smiled down at her.

"I've been wanting to kiss you ever since the first day I saw you," he whispered. She needed romance in her life, and Marcia knew she would have him in her arms again.

Chapter 7

Stephane held Marcia near his body for the next hour while they flew over the green fields. "I never want to let you go. I could snuggle with you all day," he whispered in her ear as they descended toward a green pasture. *I haven't felt alive like this in years. I'm so fortunate to have met her,* he thought. He didn't want to leave her side, afraid that it was just a dream. He texted Andre from his phone and told him where to meet them when they landed. He told him to find a spot and then set up the blanket and the picnic basket his mother had prepared for them. They were at the end of their balloon ride. He held her tighter against his body, not wanting to let go. He couldn't wait to see what would happen during the rest of the date. He had finally kissed her, and now he craved more.

"Hold on tight. We are about to land," Julian shouted to them as he maneuvered the balloon down to the ground. Stephane tightened his grip on both the basket and Marcia. He saw that her knuckles were white from gripping the basket. *She must be afraid or nervous,* he thought.

"It's okay. Don't be scared. I'll be right here to catch you," he reassured her, then laughed. The basket hit the ground smoothly.

"Whoohoo! I'm glad that's over. I prefer it to be in the air. I wasn't so sure about the landing," she said as a nervous laugh escaped her. Her giggles were sweet sounds to his ears.

"Don't worry! I'm right here, and I wouldn't let anything happen to you. Julian knows his stuff," he reassured her, smiling her way.

He took a step away from her so they could disembark. He gripped the side of the basket and jumped out over the rim, landing firmly on his feet, then stretched out his arms to help Marcia down. Grabbing her by the waist, he lifted her up and swung her over the border of the basket. He held her close against his torso for a moment, not wanting to put her down. Unable to help himself, he stole another kiss. He noticed her cheeks turn pink for just an instant. As she blushed, she cast her eyes to the side. He unwillingly released her, trying not to laugh, then said, "Just give me a minute. I just want to thank Julian, and I'll be right back."

"No problem! I'm not going anywhere." she replied. Stephane winked at her, and she blushed again. He pursed his lips together to stop himself from laughing again, causing her to turn her face away from him. He watched as she stepped away from the balloon. She pointed toward the car, where Andre was waiting patiently. Stephane nodded, then turned his attention to Julian. He hurried, as he didn't want to be separated from her for too long.

"Thanks for an extraordinary flight, Julian. I'll definitely do this again," he said as he shook Julian's hand.

Stephane quickly returned to Marcia's side and stood in front of her, only inches from her body. He needed to touch her. He positioned his hands on her hips and looked down at her. "That was so much fun. I enjoyed it even more because you were by my side. Now, are you hungry?" he asked her softly.

She nodded at him, and he glanced at his chauffeur, who was standing by the Bentley.

"I prepared everything by the oak tree over there," Andre said to Stephane.

"Thank you, Andre," Stephane said, then nodded at him. Andre then returned to sit inside the car.

"Since it's such a nice evening, I figured we could have a picnic instead of being stuck in a stuffy restaurant with a bunch of people. There will be fewer interruptions, so we can talk...and I don't want to share you with anyone. I hope that's okay with you," he told her, all the while thinking that the real reason he didn't want to go to a public place was because he wanted to be alone with her so he might be able to steal kisses.

"Boy, you are full of surprises, aren't you? I think a picnic is perfect," she replied, and he noticed her eyes light up.

"Andre set us up under a tree by the river. Shall we go?" he asked, although he didn't want to release her. He held on to her an extra second longer, then took a step back. He extended his hand to her, and she immediately placed her hand in his palm. The mere contact of her skin against his was electric. He squeezed her hand lightly and led the way, not saying a word until they arrived at the edge of the blanket. Andre had brought a couple of pillows for their comfort, and the picnic basket had been placed on one of the corners of the blanket. Marcia stood at the edge of the blanket for a moment, then took a step forward.

"Mmmm! I really hope there is something delicious in that basket. I don't know about you, but I'm starving," she said, chuckling.

"To tell you the truth, I don't know what's in it, but I know it can't be as delicious as you," he said. He watched as she walked forward and sat on one of the pillows. He followed, sitting down next to her. She was so close that he could barely concentrate on anything but her. *Keep your desires in check; otherwise you might scare her away*, he told himself. He loved her long eyelashes, the curves of her face. and her delicate hands. She cleared her throat and pointed at the basket, and her actions brought him back from his daydream. He reached over and pulled the basket closer to them.

"Let's check and see what we have," he said as he opened it. First he unfolded a small, checkered cloth and placed it in front of them, and then he began taking every item out, setting them out on the cloth.

"We have cheese, grapes, smoked salmon, a baguette, salami, and, best of all, a bottle of white wine," he told her as he untied the corkscrew from the top of the basket and proceeded to open the bottle of wine. She grabbed two wine glasses and waited patiently for him to pour the beverage.

"Thank you for a delightful evening. This is absolutely divine," she said softly.

"It was my pleasure. I hope this is the first of many evenings together," Stephane said, and they both took a sip of their wine. He leaned over and kissed her again. Her lips were silky, and she tasted sweet. He never wanted to leave her side. After pulling back from her, he changed his mind and decided to steal one more kiss. This one was more profound, and after their lips separated, his tongue slid down the side of her neck, stopping at her shoulder as he gave it a wet kiss.

"Let's eat," he managed say as he pulled away from her. He knew he had to stop because all he wanted to do was feel his mouth all over her body, and these thoughts were making him aroused. She didn't say a word. He grabbed the baguette and broke it in two, then passed her a piece. Then he took a knife and cut a piece of cheese and salami for her. For the next hour they enjoyed each other's company, kissed, and talked about their plans to see each other again. Time flew by, and before they knew it, the stars were out and the moon was illuminating their special rendezvous. He held her close for most of the evening while they leaned against the trunk of the tree and talked, with him stealing kisses when he had an opportunity. She never resisted, so he was pleased. The wind blew colder air their way, and he noticed that she was rubbing her arms to warm up. He wrapped his arms tighter around her.

"It's getting late. As much as I don't want it to end..." Stephane said reluctantly.

"I understand. We have to go. You have a long day of work waiting for you tomorrow," Marcia said. She reached over and started putting things away in the basket while he folded the blanket. They walked back to the car, where Andre was waiting to take them home.

As they drove down the street where Marcia's hotel was located, sadness came over Stephane. He didn't want to leave her side. He looked out his window at her hotel and wondered if she would invite him in. Andre stopped the car in front of the building, then shut the engine off.

"I'll walk you to the door," Stephane told her as he reached for the door handle.

"Why don't we have one last glass of wine at the bar before you leave," she said calmly. He stopped and smiled at her.

"I'd love to," he replied, quickly opening his door and hopping out to go meet her on the other side of the vehicle. He watched as she gracefully got out of the car.

"Come on. Let's go in. It's chilly," she said without looking at him, and then, like she had the previous night, she started walking in front of him, but this time he followed her in. Stephane turned and motioned to Andre with his hand, telling him to wait. Andre also knew that if his boss didn't show up in an hour, he could leave the keys and return home. Stephane quickened his pace to catch up to Marcia. He placed his hand on her lower back and adjusted his pace to match hers. Stephane opened the door for her so she could enter the foyer of the hotel, but she stopped walking and placed her hand flat on his chest, then looked him straight in his eyes.

His heart stopped beating for an instant as she softly said, "We can have a drink at the bar over here, or we could order room service to my room. Your choice," She gave him the most devilish smirk, as she already knew his response. They stood side by side, eyes locked on each other.

"That's easy, room service," was all he could respond to her. She took his hand and led him up the stairs. When they arrived at her door, he waited for her to unlock it, still unable to believe that he was there with her. Deep down he hoped that something would happen between them, but he would restrain himself. He didn't want to lose her by being too forward. He felt his heart race at the thought of being alone with her in her room. She pulled her key out of her bag and placed it in the keyhole, slowly opening the door.

The minute the door opened, she turned and smiled at him. Stephane couldn't help himself anymore. He slipped his hand around her waist and pulled her against him. With his left foot, he kicked the door shut, and then his lips came crashing down on hers. She didn't push him away. He heard her pocketbook fall to the ground as he felt her arms wrap around his neck. She moaned, and it drove him wild. He felt his groin surge. She pushed away from him just enough for her to slowly unbutton every button of his shirt while she stared at him. She slithered her fingertips down to his belt and unbuckled it. Stephane just watched in disbelief as his erection responded to her touch. She stepped backwards toward the bed. Pulling her blouse over her head, she exposed her bare breasts to him. He followed without objection. She came forward and put her wet mouth on his neck, causing him to tremble with desire. When she pushed his shirt off of his shoulders and licked his chest and nipples, he knew she was his for the night. As her bare breasts rubbed against his body, he was consumed with lust. He scooped her up in his arms and carried her the rest of the way to her bed, unable to wait any longer to explore and savor her.

* * *

Marcia woke up the next morning at dawn with a man's arm spread across her chest, but for once she was in no hurry to move or get out of the bed. It wasn't a service; she wasn't getting paid to be there. She just wanted to stay. She relished in this moment next to Stephane, snuggling closer to him because she needed it to last as long as possible, just in case there wouldn't be another night.

She turned her head slightly and looked up at him. His eyes were closed, his lips were parted a bit, and he was sleeping soundly. She listened to his breathing and licked her lips as she admired his features—his broad shoulders, his facial shadow, and the hip that was half exposed from the sheet. She lay on her back quietly, then glanced out the window as she thought about how she would have to call Tiffany to tell her all about Stephane. She smiled at the thought. A few minutes went by before the grip of his arm suddenly tightened around her belly.

"A penny for your thoughts. What are you smiling about?" Stephane inquired, and she felt his lips on the side of her neck. She wasn't about to tell him, so she told a little white lie.

"I was just about to get up and order coffee from downstairs. I was wondering what you would like to eat for breakfast." she lied. She felt his hand rub her belly and slip between her upper thighs. She moaned, but it didn't stop him.

"I'm not difficult. I'll just have you for breakfast," he murmured in her ear, then nibbled on her earlobe with his mouth. She whimpered softly.

"Hmmm! That's easy," she answered just as his other hand came up to cup her breast. She turned toward him and enveloped his mouth with hers. She straddled his body, unable to wait to feel him inside her again.

The next thing she knew, it was noontime and they were still sitting in bed. She hummed a song as she ate the last bite of the croissant they had ordered earlier from room service, after their lovemaking had finally ended.

"What time should I pick you up tonight?" she heard him ask. Turning to face him, she moved her body and mounted his stomach. She tilted her head, then grinned at him. He lay flat on his back as he wrapped his large hands around her hips.

"It depends. What did you have in mind?" she asked him flirtatiously, never taking her eyes off of him.

"It's all up to you, honey. I just need a few hours this afternoon to clear my desk, and then I'm all yours," he said as he lifted himself up and snuggled his face between her breasts. She felt his moist mouth kissing her cleavage.

"Well, I suppose that the sooner you leave, the sooner you can come back," she teased him, slapping his arm lightly and trying to move away from him, but he held on to her tightly and kept kissing her.

"I'm returning to Paris tomorrow. I need to pack and..." She trailed off. She didn't want to return to Paris; she wanted to stay in his arms. He immediately stopped kissing her, then embraced her, giving her a serious look.

"Why don't you stay a few more days? I want to spend more time with you," he asked her with a frown.

"I can't. I really have to..." She trailed off again, then bowed her head. She knew she would rather be with him, but at the same time, she didn't want to look too eager to be with him. The only thing that saddened her was that he wouldn't be with her if she returned to Paris. But how long could their relationship really last? The minute she was gone, it would be over. Nothing ever lasted; she had learned that early on. Every time she liked a guy, he would disappear, so now she refused to get her hopes up only to have them shattered by Stephane.

"I'll be here at six-thirty. We will talk about this then. Is that okay?" he asked. He seemed disappointed that she was leaving, but they still had one more night. He pushed the sheet from his body and stood up.

What a fine physique that man has, she thought as she examined his body from head to toe. *His butt is firm, and his—get your mind out of the gutter,* she thought.

"That's perfect. I'll be waiting right here," she answered, smirking as she followed him with her eyes as he gathered his clothes from the floor. She observed his every movement as he put them on. He looked up and saw her eyeing him, then gave her a devilish look.

"I have to leave now; otherwise I might never go. The people at work must be curious as to where the hell I am," he said, laughing. She removed the sheet from around her body and went to stand beside him. He pulled her close to his body and kissed her passionately. She didn't want to let him go. He slapped her on her butt, then took her hand in his as they walked toward the door of her room.

"I'll see you soon...just a few hours, okay?" he uttered quietly, then planted another kiss on her lips.

"I can't wait," she said, chuckling.

She opened the door, and he stepped out. She watched him walk down the hallway and disappear down the stairs. She closed the door and leaned her back against it. Raising her hand to her mouth, she closed her eyes. Even now she could feel his last kiss.

* * *

Stephane strolled back to the Bentley that was parked in the hotel lot, his head bowed low. He didn't want Marcia to leave and return to Paris. Paris seemed so far from him, even though it was only a couple of hours away. His work was in Epernay. He sat in his car and pondered how he could solve this problem. He tapped his fingers on the steering wheel and scratched his head. *I could always work from my apartment in Paris. I've done it before. It won't be ideal, but Papa will accept my decision if I explain the situation. I want to spent time with this woman,* he thought. He would have to come back to Epernay periodically, but it wasn't that far by train. He would ask his father for permission, and it would no longer be a problem, especially after his father found out that there was a special woman involved. He reached over to start his car, then began to sing a tune with the music on the radio. He drove as fast as he could to get back to the vineyard, then traveled directly up the road that led to the building where his father's office was located. He needed the solution resolved so he could unwind the knot he felt in his stomach from thinking of losing Marcia to Paris.

He took the stairs two at a time as he went up to his father's bureau, not wanting to wait for the elevator. After taking a deep breath in the hallway, he went through the entrance.

"Bonjour, Monsieur LaRoche," Celine, his father's secretary, said as he passed by her desk and went straight to the office door.

"Bonjour, Mademoiselle Celine," he replied without stopping.

"Bonjour, Stephane. Where have you been hiding all morning? I was expecting you earlier," his father said as he looked up from his paperwork. Stephane approached the mahogany desk and sat in one of the black leather chairs that faced his father. He had always thought that his father's work in the office didn't reflect what he loved to do. His father sat in this big chair going over stats, but Stephane knew he wanted to do manual work instead of contracts. His passion was to work with his hands. It was just the opposite with Stephane, who loved to deal with the agreements, people, and negotiations. One of the perks of Stephane's job was that he had the best of both worlds—he could travel, work, and come back home to his family anytime.

"Oh, I've been around." He snickered at his dad, who burst out laughing and put his pen down to look at Stephane.

"Who is she? I know that when I don't see you come in early, it usually pertains to a woman. And the unshaved whiskers..." his father said, still chuckling. Stephane's hand went up, and he rubbed his chin.

"I can't hide anything from you, can I? You are right. This one is special, and I like her a lot. That's all I'm going to say for now," he replied. A bit embarrassed, he hadn't taken the time to shave and shower before coming to see his father. He turned his head to the right, grinning as he thought of Marcia.

"I hope you're right. It would be nice if you settled down. Why don't you bring her over so we can meet her? I'll have your mother cook her a meal. That alone will keep her here," he said, still smiling at his son.

"That's what I wanted to talk to you about," he said, feeling his heart begin to beat faster. Stephane kneaded his hands together as he pressed on with the conversation.

"So, tell me about her," his dad said as he sat back in his chair and smiled.

"I met her on my way back from my trip abroad a few weeks ago. She is an American who is visiting Paris for a year. She is here in Epernay, but she is returning to Paris tomorrow. I want to continue seeing her, so I thought I might work from my apartment for a little while so I can get to know her a little better; otherwise—" He was interrupted by his father.

"I'm sure you already know her well," his father joked teasingly. Stephane couldn't help but chuckle under his breath, embarrassed that his father knew him that well.

"That shouldn't be a problem. Remember, you must come to visit occasionally, or your mother will have my head on a platter," his father told him. Stephane beamed broadly at the thought of spending more time with Marcia.

"Thanks, Papa. I suppose I have some work to finish up and some packing to do before I go. I'll leave you to your work," he said contentedly, then exited his father's office. A feeling of relief and happiness swept over him.

Stephane was sitting at his desk, catching up on work and gathering documents to bring with him, when he looked at his Cartier watch and saw that it was four-thirty. *Time passes quickly*, he thought. He dropped the last of his paperwork into his case and stood up, then hurried out the office and headed in the direction of his house so he could go home and shower. He couldn't wait to hold Marcia in his arms again.

Stephane was in his bedroom when someone knocked at the door. He didn't bother stopping from his task, as he had no time to waste. He continued gathering his belongings, knowing that it was either his sister or his mother at the door.

"Come in," he answered as he placed the last pieces of clothing in a suitcase. He looked up as Etienne strolled in. She sat on the edge of his bed, next to his suitcase.

"I hear you're leaving to return to Paris and that this time it has to do with a woman. She must be exceptional for you to leave Epernay," she casually said. Stephane stopped what he was doing to glance at her.

"Gee, news spreads fast around here. Does Maman know yet?" he asked her. He didn't care if the world knew; nothing could change his mood. Etienne nodded his way, her eyebrows raised.

"She's happy for you. She wants you to bring the girl over so we can all meet her. We are keeping our fingers crossed that maybe she..." Etienne trailed off as she began to zip up his suitcase for him.

Stephane placed his hands on his hips and burst out laughing as he shook his head.

"I just met her. Give me a break and some time to get to know her a little, will you? No secrets around here, I swear. I'll talk to Maman before I leave, and don't circulate any rumors, will you?" he asked as he lifted the suitcase off of the bed and placed it next to his bedroom door.

"So, you like her? Tell me about her. It must be serious for you to work out of the apartment. She's the girl from the vineyard the other day, isn't she? Why don't you invite her to my engagement party? You do need an escort anyway," she said as she poked at him. He turned around and looked at her playfully.

"Questions...too many questions. Her name is Marcia Philips, and she's amazing. Now give me some time before I have to introduce her to the rest of the family. I don't want her to run away just yet," he said. He knew his family would love Marcia, but he didn't want to scare her away. He leaned over and kissed his sister's cheek.

"Now, behave while I'm gone. Love you," Stephane told her as he picked up his suitcase.

He took a step forward to depart from his room, but his sister spoke to him once again. "Think about bringing her to the party, okay?" He smiled at her, but didn't say a word. He put one foot in front of the other, then hurried downstairs to speak to his mother before going off to meet Marcia.

Chapter 8

Marcia sat on one of the benches outside the main door of the hotel, her eyes glued to the long driveway as she waited for Stephane to come pick her up. She glanced at her watch again and saw that it was past six-thirty. She bit her lower lip and clutched her handbag tightly. *Maybe he's not coming,* she thought. *Maybe he forgot or changed his mind—For God's sake, Marcia, he's only ten minutes late. Relax. He'll be here soon.* Her right knee bounced up and down as she trotted her leg.

She stood up when she saw Stephane's car drive up. She exhaled, relieved that he had come. He drove right up to her, the passenger window rolled down. She took a step forward and leaned in to look at him.

"Good evening, beautiful. Did you miss me?" she heard Stephane ask enthusiastically.

"So sorry I'm late. I got caught up with work," he told her. She opened the door and sat down. His tardiness was forgiven when she saw him.

"It's okay, and yes, I missed you," she answered, giggling. He reached over, cupped his hands around her face, and kissed her passionately. She had to pull away to catch her breath.

"Well, you did miss me, didn't you?" she said as she buckled her seatbelt and placed her hand on his right upper leg. She turned to look at him again, and he had a smirk on his face.

"What? Why are you grinning at me that way?" she asked playfully as she squeezed his leg lightly, not taking her eyes off of him. He didn't answer right away. Instead, he reached over and pulled her to him. His lips came bearing down on hers again, his tongue exploring every part of her mouth. Heat exploded between her legs instantly.

Finally, he released her and said, "I've been dreaming of doing that all day." He took his foot off of the brakes, and the car started to roll forward.

"I have a surprise for you," he said as he drove down the driveway.

"Not another surprise! I can't wait. Tell me," she coaxed him, but he didn't answer right away. He turned to face her.

"I hope you won't get upset or think I'm too forward, but I decided to work from Paris for a while so we can continue our relationship. I didn't want to be that far from you. Is that all right with you?" he asked in a calm voice. Marcia was stunned for a moment, speechless. She hadn't expected him to change his life for her. Her mouth opened to respond, but nothing came out. She couldn't think. She just stared at him for a long minute. Joy filled her body. Neither one spoke a word. He focused on his driving, looking straight ahead.

"You don't approve. I'm sorry. I thought... Forget I mentioned it," he whispered, and then she saw disappointment in his eyes. It brought her back to her senses.

"You sure do know how to surprise a girl. I think that's a fabulous idea. I really would love to spend more time with you, especially in Paris," she told him, then leaned over and gently kissed him on the cheek.

"Really? There for a second, I was kind of scared that you didn't want to see that much of me anymore," he told her. He took his hand and pretended to wipe the sweat off of his forehead. She gently slapped his hand.

"Oh! Stop it!" she said while laughing at him.

"Yes, I do want to spend more time with you. I am very happy with your decision to come to Paris. Now, where are we going to eat? I haven't eaten since you left. I'm famished," she said to him, and she noticed him relax his grip on the steering wheel.

"You are always hungry! Don't they feed you at the hotel? How about I park the car downtown? Then we can walk Champagne de Avenue and decide where we want to go eat on the way," he suggested to her.

"That sounds like a plan. Let go!" she said, still in disbelief that he was coming to Paris with her. She was pleased. Maybe this was her chance to finally find a love of her own.

Isn't this what you always wanted deep down? she thought. *You need to enjoy the ride and see where it takes you.* His mood seemed to be restored, and he reached over to the volume of the radio and began to sing along with the song. It made her beam. This man made her whole being content. She watched as his shoulders swayed side to side and his fingers drummed to the sound of the beat. He had absolutely no rhythm. She couldn't help herself and started laughing uncontrollably, tears falling down her cheeks. But it didn't make him stop.

Marcia had been back in her apartment in Paris for two weeks. She was cutting vegetables for dinner at the counter in her tiny kitchen, preparing dinner for Stephane, when her cell phone rang.

She put the knife down, glanced down at the caller ID, and immediately picked up her phone. It was her friend Tiffany. Marcia hadn't talked to her since she had left Epernay.

"Allo," she answered, happy to hear from her best friend. Marcia had been so busy with her new lover that she hadn't had time to talk to her.

"Oh my God! You sound just like a real Frenchwoman," Tiffany said, laughing.

"How are you, Tiffany? I've been meaning to call you, but I've been so occupied with..." She stopped mid-sentence. Marcia still hadn't told her about Stephane.

"With what, or should I say who? Only a man would stop you from calling me," Tiffany said. Marcia leaned her back against the counter and laughed out loud. She wiped her hands on her apron. It was nice to hear from her girlfriend; she missed her.

"I can't lie; you know me too well. I did meet someone. His name is Stephane LaRoche, and he is unbelievable. He is handsome, kind, and considerate," she said as she reached over and grabbed her wineglass, taking a sip of the drink.

"Ohh! Do tell me more! Does he have a friend I could meet? Is he rich? Is he great in bed?" Tiffany teased Marcia.

"I miss you so much. I wish you would come visit me. You could stay with me, and we could have girl talks like we used to," Marcia told her friend.

"That is why I'm calling. I've decided to come by for a visit. I do deserve some time off, and I have never been to Paris. What do you think?" Tiffany asked her. Marcia almost dropped the phone as she jumped for joy.

"Yes, that is a superb idea. When will you be arriving? I have so much to tell you. I can't wait to see you," she answered instantly.

"I'll book a flight for the day after tomorrow. I know it's short notice, but you know how I am when I decide something. I do things on the spur of the moment. I hope you don't mind me popping in unexpected." Tiffany sounded excited to come see her.

"No, no. That's perfect. It will give me time to get a few things ready. I am so thrilled you decided to come. I will show you around town, my dear, and you can meet my new beau. You can let me know what you think. There is so much to do here, and the shopping... ooh la la!" Marcia told her, then grinned at the thought of Stephane meeting her best friend.

"All right, I just wanted to let you know. Now I must run. I have some last minute shopping to do. You know how I always must look my best. I'll email you my schedule as soon as I book," Tiffany replied cheerfully.

"Please do that. I'll be waiting for you up at the airport. We will have lots to talk about. I'm so excited you are coming. See you soon. Aurevoir," Marcia said, laughing at the thought of having her friend around for a while.

"Aurevoir," Tiffany answered back mockingly, and then Marcia heard a click meaning the line was dead.

Two days later Marcia waited patiently for Tiffany to arrive at the immigration doors of the Charles de Gaulle Airport. Every time the doors opened, Marcia would scan the area for her friend, eyeing every person that came through the doors. She stood at the front line, by the railing of the exit. Once again the doors opened, and then Marcia saw her. She jumped up and down, waving her hands in Tiffany's direction. Marcia called out, "Tiffany, over here." Tiffany acknowledged her by lifting her chin up and waving.

As always, Tiffany's attire was flawless, and all eyes were on her. Marcia shook her head and admired the friend who taught her everything she knew about fashion. She was dressed in a low-cut tight black dress, three-inch Valentino black heels, and a red Louis Vuitton shawl that was wrapped around her shoulders. Her hair was twirled in a bun on top of her head, and her makeup looked fresh. She looked fabulous. A porter was following her with her bags. Marcia approached her with quick steps, then opened her arms. They hugged and kissed each other on the cheeks.

"I'm so happy you are here. Let me look at you," Marcia said, moving a few feet back but still holding her hand. Tiffany spun around and laughed.

"You really don't look like you just flew a seven and-a-half-hour flight. I really hate you!" Marcia told her as she admired her. They both laughed.

"Darling, you're not bad looking yourself. I did teach you well. Paris must agree with you, or is it the new beau in your life," Tiffany teased as she looked Marcia over from head to toe. Marcia placed her arm through Tiffany's and guided her toward the exit. The porter followed them with the suitcases.

"How long are you staying? Are you moving here too? You brought a whole wardrobe!" Marcia made fun of her as she pointed at all the luggage. Tiffany shrugged her shoulders.

"Hell no! But as you should know, I do need to be prepared for all occasions. We are in Paris! You never know what you might need. I may meet a wealthy Frenchman too," she responded, smiling as they walked arm and arm out the terminal, on their way to catch a cab to return to Marcia's home.

A couple of hours later they were chatting as if they had never been apart from each other, catching up on all the news. They sat across from each other on Marcia's balcony, drinking a bottle of white wine and munching on nuts. They watched the people stroll on the street.

Marcia had always considered Tiffany the sister she never had, and she was also her confidante. They shared everything.

"We've talked about everything under the sun except mystery man. Now that we are settled in, give me the scoop. I know you are dying to tell more," Tiffany said as she took another handful of nuts, popped a few in her mouth, and smiled. Marcia closed her eyes momentarily as a vision of Stephane came to her mind. Her heart warmed at the thought of him. She took a long breath and exhaled as a broad smile came across her face.

"I first saw Stephane on the plane ride coming over here, but I ignored him even though I thought he was fine. I had told myself I would not look at another man for a year. Then, you won't believe this!" she squealed as she sat at the edge of her chair and clapped her hands. Tiffany listened attentively.

"I met him again in Paris, and then again at a vineyard I went to visit, which, to my amazement, belongs to his family. I tried to disregard him, and I rebuffed his invitations repeatedly, but he kept coming back. I think it was faith. He's tall, he has blue eyes, he's funny and wealthy, and I think I love him," she blurted out. Her hand went to her chest as she took another breath.

"You think you love him? Hmmm, that's totally out of character for you. Didn't you listen to what I told you before you left? Do not fall in love with a Parisian," Tiffany responded calmly. She tilted her head at Marcia, and her eyebrows rose as she looked at her. Marcia slowly nodded her head up and down without saying a word. They both burst out laughing at the same time, and Marcia had a pain in her side by the time they stopped.

"So when do I get to meet this prince charming?" Tiffany asked, still trying to regain her composure. "Considering what I just heard from you, I approve."

Marcia put her hand up. "Hold that thought," she said.

"As a matter of fact, we are meeting him for dinner in about..." Marcia raised her arm and read the time on her Chopard watch, then said, "I'd say two hours or so, at around nine o'clock. I thought we could go to one of my favorite restaurants; it's called Le Fouquet. It's located on the famous Champs Elysees. That way, you get to see a few of the famous sites along the way."

"That sounds delightful," Tiffany answered. She gulped down the last drops of her wine, then refilled her glass.

"It's a casual restaurant, but if you want, we can freshen up now so we can leave earlier and do some window shopping along the way. We could maybe buy a few things before dinner," Marcia suggested to her.

"Yes, I think we should do that. I wouldn't want him to meet me when I look like this," she said, chuckling. They both stood up, grabbed their wine glasses, and walked toward the bedroom to change for an evening out on the town, and maybe a little browsing in the stores.

An hour later Marcia and Tiffany had revived themselves, and they caught a cab to Champs Elysee Avenue. The driver dropped them off on a side street next to the Louis Vuitton building. They strolled down the brick sidewalks in high heels, walking arm in arm as they admired the handbags and shoes featured in the window.

"Let's go in. I'm dying to see the new fashion. We have time, right?" Tiffany asked excitedly.

Marcia glanced at her watch and nodded. "The restaurant is just across the street. We still have an hour before our reservation. Come on. Let's check it out!" she answered, then walked to the main glass doors and entered one of the most famous stores in Paris.

"Bonsoir, Mademoiselles." An employee dressed in all black greeted them at the door. "If you need any help, please do not hesitate to ask," he said, smiling at them.

"Merci, Monsieur," Marcia answered as she and Tiffany examined the pocketbooks on the shelves. They commented to each other on different items, but neither of them found anything to their liking on the first floor, so they proceeded to the second floor, where the clothing department and shoes were located. Tiffany went up the escalator first, holding on to the railing while she chatted away. When Marcia was halfway up, she turned her head to look down at the patrons down shopping below her, shopping. Marcia noticed a tall man at one of the counters that caught her attention. She could only partially see him because a pillar was blocking her view and only saw him from the side. She stared at him, intrigued. *I think I know that man*, she thought. *If only he would turn around so I could see his face.*," Marcia leaned forward for a better look.

"Are you coming?" she heard Tiffany say. She had stopped at the landing a few steps up from her.

"Tiffany, come here," Marcia told her, and friend came to stand near her. "Do you see that man in the blue suit at the counter? He looks familiar. Do you know him?" she murmured to Tiffany while keeping her eyes on him.

Tiffany looked at him quickly, then turned to face Marcia. "Isn't one man enough for you?" she joked while Marcia observed him.

"Tiffany, I'm serious. Look at him. I can't see his face, but I think I know him," Marcia told her. She pointed at him just as the man turned around to examine another bag. Marcia recognized him instantly. *Those deep-set black eyes, the full mouth, and the mustache—how could I forget him?* She glanced at Tiffany, who was as white as chalk. She had gripped the railing to steady herself from fainting.

"Is that..." Marcia asked her, and Tiffany nodded without a word. Marcia grabbed her by the arm, and they sprinted away from the stairs. They were all the way at the far end of the store before either of them spoke. As they stood behind a rack of dresses, they peeked at the entryway of the escalator.

"What is he doing here? Son of a bitch! What are we going to do?" Tiffany asked in a low voice. Marcia noticed that Tiffany's hands were still shaking, even though some of the color had reappeared on her face.

"I don't know. He must be here on business. Are you sure it's him?" Marcia asked again, hoping they were wrong.

"How can I forget what that bastard did?" Tiffany answered as she inhaled deeply. Marcia took her hand in hers, trying to reassure her that everything would be okay.

"Don't worry; everything is fine. I'm here. He won't do anything rash. Now, let's find our way out of this store and get to the restaurant. It will be all right. I won't leave you alone, okay?" Marcia said to her as anger built in her gut. She wanted to go downstairs and punch the crap out of that man, but right now she had to take care of her friend. Marcia looked around for another way to get downstairs. *I hope he doesn't come upstairs; otherwise... What are we going to do?* Marcia thought as she took a few steps toward a room that was adjacent to where they were standing.

"Over there; let's go," Marcia told Tiffany. She pointed to an elevator sign that was located at the other end of the second room. Marcia grabbed Tiffany's arm, and they both hurried in the direction of the lift. Marcia extended her hand and pushed the button several times. Tiffany looked over shoulder and scanned the area.

Marcia touched her arm lightly and said, "It's okay. He won't hurt you. We are in a public place, so he won't do anything. We are safe. I promise." Marcia said trying to put her mind at rest. Finally, the elevator doors opened, and within seconds the girls were inside, on their way downstairs. They marched out of the store as fast as they could, avoiding the front counter, where that man had been standing. They took long strides down the avenue, only to slow down when they were across the street. Marcia's heart was beating fast. Tiffany kept turning around to scrutinize the people behind her. Marcia knew Tiffany was frightened.

Marcia could see the red awnings of the restaurant up ahead, which caused her to sigh with relief. "The restaurant is right here," she said, then pointed ahead. "It's okay. He's gone. It's a large city, and he won't find us. Now, let's relax and have a nice dinner. Let's forget we ever saw him," Marcia told Tiffany, who seemed a bit more composed than earlier, but she still turned around to take one last look behind her when they arrived at the entrance of Fouquet's restaurant.

"Okay, thanks. I'm sorry, but I just can't forget how he..." Tiffany mumbled to her.

Marcia reached over and gave her a hug. "I know, baby. You don't have to say a word. I understand. He won't hurt you. I'm here for you," Marcia told her, then took her hand in hers and squeezed it. They went in the entrance of the eatery where they had reservations. They were greeted at the door by an older gentleman in a suit.

"Bonsoir, do you have reservations?" he asked politely.

"Bonsoir, yes, the name is under LaRoche, party of three," Marcia answered him quickly. She turned her head to take one last look in the direction of the Louis Vuitton store, but the man was nowhere to be seen.

"This way, Mademoiselles," he said, and they proceeded to follow him toward a table in the back, where they were then seated. The Fouquet was a historical restaurant that served French cuisine. All of the walls were paneled with oak wood from the floor up to the ceiling, and they were covered with pictures of various sights in Paris. The tables had white tablecloths with red chairs, and crystal glasses were placed on top. Chandeliers hung from the ceilings. Waiters dressed in black clothes and black aprons excellently served the patrons.

After they had been seated and were given menus, Marcia grabbed the alcohol menu and opened it, reading the selection of cocktails.

"How about a stiff drink? It will calm our nerves while we wait for Stephane. Does that sound good to you?" Marcia asked Tiffany, who hadn't said much since they had sat down. Tiffany nodded. The waiter arrived at their table a few moments later.

"Bonsoir, can I get you ladies a drink to start off with this evening while you wait for the rest of your party?" he asked them pleasantly.

Marcia placed the menu down on the table, then looked up at him. She smiled at him and said, "We will have two dry Vodka Martinis with a twist of lemon. No olives, please."

"I will be right back with those drinks and some bread," he answered, then turned around and left them alone. Marcia watched as he walked away, and her mind drifted to the previous year, to the night she had heard a knock on her door at three in the morning.

Marcia got up from her bed to see who was knocking at the door. When she looked through the peephole, her heart dropped to the floor. She swung the door open just in time to catch Tiffany, who had fallen after her legs had given out. She dragged Tiffany to her sofa in the living room, then sat her down. *Tiffany's red dress was torn at the shoulder, her hair was tousled, and her face was worst of all. One of her eyes was black and almost swollen shut. Dried blood was on her nose and at the corners of her mouth. Marcia could tell she had been crying, as her makeup was smudged all over her face.*

"Oh my God! Tiffany, are you all right? What happened? Who did this to you? We need to go to the hospital. I'll call the police and an ambulance," *Marcia blurted out all at once. But Tiffany shook her head as her body trembled uncontrollably.*

"No, you can't call! I'll be fine. I just need to rest. I don't think anything is broken," *Tiffany answered as tears streamed down her cheeks. Marcia leaned forward and embraced her tightly, crying with her.*

"I'll run you a hot bath and get you some clean clothes. It will make you feel better. You can stay here, but then we will have a talk about what happened," *Marcia told her.*

In the days that had followed, Marcia had learned that a wealthy client had slapped Tiffany around during sex, and then he had beaten her when she tried to fight him off. She had been able to escape when he fell asleep later that evening. It had taken Tiffany ten days to recover at her home before she could return to her studies. She had had nightmares every night for several months afterward. The man had left her with a scar on her eyelid from the incident— a reminder she would never be able to forget. He had never been arrested for the assault, as he was a client from the escort service and it would have exposed Tiffany, which she didn't want. A few months later Tiffany had pointed out that bastard to Marcia at an event they had attended together. Marcia had never forgotten that face; it had been engraved in her mind forever.

Now they were sitting in a fine restaurant in Paris, and the man was there, in the same city. Why? Was he vacationing? Was he there on business? Marcia didn't know, but she knew that if he came near Tiffany again, she would find the strength to kill him.

Chapter 9

Stephane felt a bit nervous as he walked toward the restaurant, especially since he was meeting Marcia's best friend. He took one last look in the rearview mirror, then quickly looked at his watch. It was almost half past the hour, which meant he was running late. As soon as he parked, he got out of the car, quickening his pace. Marcia had told him that Tiffany was her closest friend, and he had hoped that he could make a good impression on her, but now he was late. Deep down he knew everything would be fine, but he couldn't help but worry. *I hope Tiffany likes me; otherwise... But what if she doesn't? Oh God, stop it!* He took his hands out of his pantsuit pockets as he approached the front door of The Fouquet. Swinging the door open, he stepped inside and gave his name to the Maître D, who immediately escorted Stephane to the back of the restaurant, where his table was waiting. There she was, sipping a martini and sitting at a table next to a beautiful woman. He smiled at the sight of Marcia, who was wearing a low-cut white dress that showed her breasts just enough to tease him. She returned his smile when she saw him.

"There you go, Monsieur. Enjoy your evening," the Maître D said to him as he placed another menu on the table.

"Merci," Stephane replied. He didn't sit down right away, instead taking a side step and leaning down toward Marcia to kiss her on the cheek. He briefly inhaled the floral scent that he liked so much, and it momentarily calmed him. After he pulled away, he extended his hand to Tiffany to greet her.

"Bonsoir, I apologize for my lateness. I was detained with a client. I'm Stephane LaRoche. You must be Tiffany. It's a pleasure to meet you. I've heard so much about you," he said as he shook her hand.

"Pleasure is all mine, but don't believe everything she told you about me," Tiffany replied flirtatiously as she casually turned her head toward Marcia. He caught Tiffany winking at Marcia in approval, and Marcia playfully slapped her hand. He pretended not to have seen it but grinned to himself. *They really are close friends,* he thought.

He backed away from the table, pulled out the chair next to Marcia, and sat down, placing his hand on her velvety knee.

"How are you enjoying Paris so far? Is this your first time?" Stephane asked as he scanned the dining area with his eyes, looking for a waiter to bring him a drink.

"Yes, it is my first time. I haven't had much time to visit yet, but I do plan on it. It's a fabulous city," she answered, then picked up her drink and finished it.

"We haven't had much time today, but tomorrow we will visit the popular sites," he heard Marcia say to him as she discreetly covered his hand with hers.

"It's one of the oldest, most beautiful cities in Europe. I hope you have fun during your stay," he told Tiffany as a server arrived at the table.

"Bonsoir, Monsieur, what can I get you to drink?" the server asked as Stephane eyed the girls' drinks.

"I'll have whatever they are having. Another round, s'il vous plait," Stephane told him.

The server nodded, said, "I'll be right back," and walked toward the bar.

"I hope you girls are hungry, because...I hate to say it, but—" Before Stephane could finish, Marcia interrupted, completing his sentence.

"Let me guess, you're famished," she said, giggling at him.

"She's getting to know me too well, I must say, especially when she knows what I'm going to say," Stephane said, and they all laughed. He squeezed Marcia's knee lightly, then grabbed his menu so he could decide what to have for dinner. They dined, talked, and got to know each other for a few hours.

At the end of the evening, Stephane paid the bill and finished the last mouthful of his cappuccino, placing the cup down on the saucer.

"Oh, before I forget..." Stephane turned to look at Marcia.

"As you know, Etienne just got engaged, and my parents are having an engagement party for her in Paris tomorrow night. It's at The Mandarin Oriental Hotel. I would like to invite Tiffany to come along with us," Stephane said, figuring Marcia might like it and that Tiffany could keep Marcia company, although he really wanted her all for himself.

"That's so thoughtful of you, but I wouldn't want to impose on a family gathering. But if you insist..." Tiffany answered, then glanced at Marcia, who smiled and nodded her head in approval.

"No, no. Believe me, it's no imposition. It might be a little boring, but the chef does make the best French food in town. You are most welcome, and you will be able to see the city from up above. It's a rooftop restaurant," Stephane answered her.

Tiffany and Marcia nodded at him. "You never know, I might find myself a Frenchman too," Tiffany joked.

"Then it's settled. With not only one but two beautiful women under my arm, I'll be the envy of the town. I will call Marcia with the details in the morning," Stephane said, looking at Marcia, who was smiling at him. Stephane knew it would be difficult to separate these two while Tiffany was in Paris.

"Now, let me drive you back to your apartment. My car is down the block," Stephane told them as he stood up to escort them out of the dining area of the restaurant. He took Marcia's delicate hand in his, and they walked out of the restaurant and down the avenue until they were at his car. They sat quietly while Stephane drove the short distance back to Marcia's place. He parked on the side of the street, right in front of her building.

"Here we are!" Stephane said as he looked at both of the ladies. He was hoping to have a minute alone with Marcia before she went inside. After shutting the car off, he glanced her way, then placed his hand on her thigh. She smiled at him.

"Could you give us a moment? I'll be right behind you," Marcia asked her friend, and then she took out the condo keys out of her bag and gave them to Tiffany.

"No problem. Take your time. It was nice meeting you, Stephane, and thank you for dinner. I shall see you tomorrow," Tiffany said as she opened the car door, and then she disappeared behind the red door of the residence.

The second the building door closed, Stephane reached over and pulled Marcia close his chest. He wrapped his arms around her shoulder and kissed her passionately, feeling the warmth of her body against his. When he heard her quietly moan, he immediately wanted to make love to her.

"I missed you today," he whispered as his kisses trailed down from her neck to her breasts. She chuckled in delight.

"I did too," she whispered, her long hair touching the side of his face, her scent invading him.

"You shouldn't wear dresses like that. It drives me wild. Too bad you have a guest. I could follow you inside, but it wouldn't be appropriate, since this is the first time I've met her. But..." he continued to say as he felt a sexual urge in his groin area. He wanted to take her right there in the front seat of his car.

"Okay, back away, tiger." Marcia laughed as she gently pushed him away, but he didn't move. "Maybe I can arrange to come over to your apartment one night...soon," she answered as she kissed the top of his head, which was nuzzled between her breasts.

She feels and smells so good, he thought.

"I would like that. I might not be able resist you too much longer," he whispered, pulling away to look at her. He softly placed his hand on her cheek and stroked it with his fingers. Closing his eyes, he enjoyed the feeling of her smooth skin. She placed her hand over his, and he opened his eyes, still continuing to explore her delicate features. With the streetlight shining down on the vehicle, he could see that she was blushing.

"It was nice of you to invite Tiffany to Etienne's party. I truly appreciate the gesture," Marcia said to him as her hand trailed down to his chest and rested there. Her contact made him want her more, so he moved closer to her.

"My pleasure! Adding one more person to the guest list is not going to make a difference at this party. Now go before I kidnap you and bring you home with me. I'll call you tomorrow," Stephane told her, but before he pulled away, he cupped his hands around her face and planted another kiss on those perfect lips.

He finally let go of her and watched as she departed from his car. She buzzed her way into the apartment to go join her friend. He sat still for a few seconds, observing her every movement, all the while not wanting to leave her side. After starting his car, he began driving down the narrow streets, thinking of how he missed not being with her every night and how he counted every minute until she would be back in his arms. *I think I'm in love with this woman. There is no other explanation for how I feel about her*, he concluded. When he arrived at home, Stephane walked to the elevator and pushed the button that would take him upstairs. He closed his eyes and inhaled; he could smell her fragrance on his shirt. He smiled.

* * *

Marcia and Tiffany spent the next morning drinking espresso coffee and eating croissants on the balcony, talking like teenage schoolgirls about Stephane.

"Your guy is absolutely a catch. He's perfect for you. You have my approval," Tiffany said. "What are we going to do about that bastard we saw last night? What if we bump into him again?" Tiffany asked.

Marcia saw Tiffany touch the scar on her eyebrow, the one he had left behind as a reminder of him, and knew she was still frightened of encountering him again.

"Tiffany, don't worry. It's a huge city. The chances of us bumping into him again are one in a million, and you are not alone. I'll be right beside you to punch the crap out of him," Marcia said, snickering.

"Okay, sorry, I was just freaking out. You are right! What are we going to wear to the engagement dinner this evening?" Tiffany asked, changing the subject.

"Let's go shopping! I could use a new dress, and I know the ideal place to take you. You will love this place. It has the latest French fashions; as a matter of fact, it has the latest world fashions. We could spend hours in there," Marcia exclaimed. She bounced in her seat at the thought of going to this megastore. When she stood up and looked at her watch, she saw that the time read ten o'clock in the morning, so they still had enough time to go look for a new dress.

"My kind of location. Let's go," Tiffany said, her eyes widening with excitement as she stood up from the table.

"All right then. Let's get changed quickly so we can get going. We can walk over and be there in less than an hour if we hurry. That should give us plenty of time to do a little damage to our expense accounts. We can grab a late lunch near there." Marcia was talking while she walked back to her bedroom, with Tiffany trailing behind her, who was jumping around eagerly. An hour later they had walked to Boulevard Haussmann and had arrived right in front of the front doors of the store. Lafayette Galleries was founded in the 19th century and was the second most popular tourist attraction, after the Eiffel Tower, in Paris. It was a seven-floor building with a stained-glass dome on the ceiling and was known for having the best fashion in all of Paris. Every floor featured famous designers from around the world.

The girls entered the store through the glass doors and walked forward upon the main floor. Marcia looked over at Tiffany, who had stopped walking. She was standing motionless, looking up in awe at the beauty of the store's dome and the many floors above.

"I've never seen anything so spectacular. The dome is...magnificent. Where do you start? You could be here for days," Tiffany said to Marcia, who started to laugh. Marcia grabbed Tiffany's arm and guided her to the women's department. They strolled past aisles and aisles of perfumes and women's accessories, heading toward the moving staircase.

"Come on! We can start in the women's section on the next floor, and then we'll make our way up to other floors. Do you have a favorite designer, because they are all under one roof?" Marcia asked, giggling as she stepped onto the escalator, Tiffany following close behind.

"I want to see everything. My God! I'm in heaven," Tiffany said as they stepped off on the first floor and began admiring the new trends from each designer. By mid-afternoon they had both found dresses for the evening event, but they were still shopping.

Marcia was standing by a rack of Yves St. Laurent fashions when she saw a man browsing the women's clothes in the next section, not too far from her. She recognized him immediately. As she held her breath and turned her back to him, her heart started to pound faster. Her eyes began darting the area for Tiffany. *What is he doing here? I need to find Tiffany right away and get her out of here. What are the chances of seeing him twice?* her mind screamed. She bent down and picked up her shopping bags, holding them tightly. When she turned to the right, relief came over her. Tiffany was browsing through a rack of shirts nearby. Marcia quickly ran over to where she was standing and gathered Tiffany's bags in her free hand.

"Tiffany," Marcia almost screamed to her. "We need to leave, now," Marcia pressed on, and then she gently pushed Tiffany to her right. Tiffany looked up briefly at Marcia, a confused look on her face, then kept examining the garments.

"Hold on one minute," she replied, unaware of what was going on. Marcia grabbed her arm tightly and shoved her. "What's the matter with you?" Tiffany asked.

Marcia pulled her arm and said, "That bastard is here. Over there! Let's get out of here before he sees us." They crouched down behind the rack. Marcia motioned for Tiffany to take a quick look in the direction of where he was shopping. She saw the color drain from Tiffany's face as she spotted him.

Under her breath, Tiffany said, "Son of a bitch! What the fuck is he doing in Paris? Do you think he is stalking us?"

"No, he isn't. You are being paranoid. He doesn't know we are here. Let's just go," Marcia insisted. Tiffany immediately dropped the item of clothing that was in her hand, and it fell on the floor. She followed Marcia, who was sprinting as quickly as possible toward the exit, not looking back once. Marcia flagged down a taxi as soon as they stepped outside of the building. They ran toward the car and sat in the back seat. Marcia sighed heavily, then turned her head to glance at Tiffany. She noticed Tiffany's hands were shaking.

"I'm not going to let him ruin my vacation. I'm going to face up to him one day and..." Tiffany's voice broke. Marcia noticed tears filling her eyes, so she reached over and squeezed her hand.

"His day will come. What goes around comes around. Don't you let him win. Now, we have a party to attend, and we are going to make the best of it," Marcia told her.

Tiffany nodded, closing her eyes for a moment. Marcia watched as Tiffany wiped the tears away from her eyes, sat up straight in the seat, and said, "Yes, let's get home and change into our beautiful dresses. We have a party to go to." As she said it, she gave Marcia a small smile.

Minutes later they were in Marcia's apartment, unpacking their purchases.

"We only have an hour before Stephane comes to pick us up, so we better hurry," Marcia said as she glanced at the clock on the wall. Both girls swiftly ran to the bedroom to get ready. An hour later Marcia was dressed in a tight fitting, bareback red dress that stopped right above her knee. Her hair was pulled up in a French twist, and her makeup couldn't have been more perfect. Tiffany had a black low-cut dress with sequins that accentuated her breasts.

"What shoes should I wear?" Marcia asked Tiffany, holding up a pair of red Valentino sandals and a pair of black Louboutin three-inch heels.

"Definitely the black ones," Tiffany answered as she sprayed perfume on. The doorbell buzzed, and Marcia hurried to the inter-com, pushing the button to let Stephane in.

"That must be Stephane. Are you ready?" Marcia asked Tiffany, who nodded. They both looked in the mirror one last time, then headed toward the front door. When Marcia opened the door, Ste-phane was standing in the doorway, a dozen red roses in his hand. He was dressed in a pinstripe black tux, a white shirt, and a blue tie. His black hair was slicked back, making him look appetizing. He smiled at her.

"Hi, gorgeous," Stephane said. He whistled at her, which made her flush, and then he leaned forward and gently kissed her lips. "These are for you." He placed the flowers in her hands.

"Thank you, you didn't have to. They are beautiful," Marcia said, then smelled their scent. He stepped inside, and she closed the door behind him.

"You look stunning. Remind me not to leave your side tonight; can't have another man taking you away," Stephane whispered to her as he followed her into the kitchen. Marcia giggled. She swiftly found a vase in the cupboard and put the roses in it.

"How was your day, girls?" Stephane asked them as he watched and waited by the counter in the kitchen.

"We had a great time shopping. I took her to Lafayette Galleries" Marcia answered while adding water to the flowers. She remembered the bastard, but pushed him away from her thoughts.

"Are you ready to leave? I don't want us to be late. Etienne does have a temper when I am not prompt," Stephane joked as he checked the time on his Rolex watch.

"We are all set. Lead the way," Marcia said cheerfully. She picked up her clutch bag and keys as they left the apartment.

They drove down St. Honore Street. Stephane pulled up in front of the Mandarin Hotel, where a valet was waiting to park the car. They stepped out of the Bentley and headed inside the hotel.

A doorman opened the front door for them and greeted them. "Bonsoir, welcome to The Mandarin Hotel," he said.

They walked through the lobby. The floors were a dark brown marble, mahogany wood paneling lined the walls, and many crystal chandeliers hung up above them. Lavishly dressed people were coming and going in all directions.

"Stunning place," Marcia told Stephane as they headed to the elevators. He rubbed her back softly while they waited for the lift. Marcia loved how he was always attentive to her. The stroke of his fingers against her skin gave her goosebumps.

"Incredible!" Tiffany added as she followed closely behind them.

"Wait until you see where the reception is held. It's on the seventh floor, on the exterior courtyard. The unroofed area has an intimate atmosphere with camellia trees and colorful flowers. And the view is spectacular! You can see for miles," Stephane said to the girls. He pushed the button for the elevator to go up. Marcia slipped her hand into his, and he turned and smiled at her. They were all quiet on the short ride up. When the doors opened, French music could immediately be heard playing in the background. A dozen tables were set up with gold and white tablecloths, along with matching, deep, lustrous yellow centerpieces of flowers. A fully stocked bar was set up to the far left, and a large selection of finger foods, including roasted duck, lobster tails, and grilled vegetables. Etienne and his parents were standing by the entrance so they could welcome their guests.

"Bonsoir, everyone. I would like you to meet Marcia and Tiffany. They are visiting from America," Stephane said to his parents and Etienne.

"Nice to meet you. Thank you for letting us celebrate this occasion with your family," Marcia said politely. She wasn't prepared to meet his family, but they seemed very pleased to see her.

"Stephane's friends are always welcome," Stephane's father said to her. Marcia saw him pat Stephane's forearm and nod as if he approved of her. Stephane took a step forward to talk to his sister, and Marcia stood next to him and waited.

Stephane scanned the room quickly. "I don't see your fiancée. Where's Mason?" he asked his sister. Maria noticed he seemed annoyed that Mason wasn't standing next to his sister.

"He just stepped out for a minute; he should be back any moment," Etienne answered her brother as she looked over his shoulder at the people who were making their way to the party.

"Okay, we are going to get a drink and mingle with the guests. I'll catch up with you guys in a bit," Stephane said, and then he escorted Marcia and Tiffany to the bar for a cocktail on the other side of the terrace.

"Mason is always late when it comes to events, but this one is their engagement party, for Christ's sake! Where the hell is he?" Stephane said in a low voice. Marcia lightly touched his arm as she stood near him.

"It's okay. I'm sure he'll be along in a few minutes. We can meet him at that time," she said, trying to soothe his irritation.

"What would you girls like to drink?" Stephane asked as they approached the bar.

"I'll have a glass of white wine...Chardonnay, if they have it. Tiffany?" Marcia asked, glancing at Tiffany.

"I'll have the same," Tiffany answered. Stephane placed the order. When it arrived, he handed both of them a glass. Marcia looked around the room, watching the many guests who were piling in.

"Would you mind finding a cocktail table? I'll join you in a few minutes. I need to use the men's room," Stephane said to Marcia.

"No problem. We'll be in that corner," Marcia answered as she pointed to the left with her chin, where there were several empty tables. Stephane leaned forward and kissed her on the cheek.

"Thanks, I'll be right back," he said, then watched the two girls walk to one of the tables. Marcia and Tiffany quickly found a tall cocktail table by the balcony. They waited patiently for Stephane to return while admiring the crowd's attire. The women sipped their wine. People were looking at them, but in a positive way. They would smile or briefly chitchat with them. Marcia noticed that people were gathering at the food station, picking out finger foods and bringing them back to their table.

"How about you hold the table and I'll go grab us a plate of those delicious appetizers I keep seeing people eating. It makes me hungry," Marcia suggested to Tiffany.

"That sounds like a marvelous idea. I'm kind of hungry anyway," Tiffany said.

Marcia took another mouthful of her wine, then placed her glass down on the table. "I'll be right back," she told her friend. She walked away from the table so she could retrieve a plate of hors d'oeuvres. As she stood at one of the food stations, she tried to decide what to put on her dish. When she was making her way down the cheese section, she fleetingly looked toward the front entrance. It took everything she had not to drop her plate. She sucked in a breath, trying to regain her composure. Her legs became weak. She stared at the man who was strolling onto the terrace, then watched in horror as he walked over to Etienne and kissed her on the cheek. Etienne smiled at him lovingly as he stood next to her and wrapped his arm around her waist.

Oh my God! This is not happening. It can't be real, Marcia told herself. She immediately turned her back to the man, carefully placing her plate down on the service table and walking away. *I need to get to Tiffany before she sees him. How am I going to deal with this problem? We need to leave before he spots Tiffany.* Within seconds she was back at their table. She swiftly put her hand on Tiffany's torso and pivoted her toward the opposite direction of where Mason was standing.

"What are you doing? Where's the food?" Tiffany asked, laughing.

"Don't turn around. Keep looking straight ahead. Listen to me. He's here," Marcia said in haste.

"Who's here? What are you talking about?" Tiffany asked, still not understanding what Marcia was trying to tell her. Tiffany took a step forward so she could turn around, but Marcia kept a hold on her arm.

"Don't turn around. Etienne's fiancée is Mason Koury. I didn't put it together until now. We need to leave before he spots us,"

Marcia whispered. Tiffany turned a few shades lighter when she realized what Marcia was telling her.

"Marcia, I'm going to throw up. What are we going to do?" Tiffany asked as her hand went to her stomach.

Marcia rubbed her hands together and bit her lip, debating back and forth on her decision, and then she spoke with confidence. "No, no, we are not going to leave. He will not hurt you. We are going to hold our heads high and face him head on. He's the one who should be afraid of us, not the other way around. We didn't do anything wrong. We will get through this together." She was trying to convince herself that everything would be okay, but she wasn't so sure just yet. She looked to see where Stephane was, but she couldn't find him. As she put her hand over Tiffany's, she stood up straight. They both looked at each other and nodded once.

"But what if he tells people about our former profession...especially to Stephane?" Tiffany asked as she grabbed her drink and gulped down the last drops of it.

"He wouldn't dare because he has as much to lose as we do. He'll keep his mouth shut. Stop worrying about it. It will be fine. Let's just stick together," Marcia said, but a wave of anger passed through her at the thought of that piece of scum ruining her chance at love and possibly hurting Stephane's sister. "I will deal with him. He will regret the day he ever met me if he tries something."

Her thoughts were interrupted when she felt a man's hand on her lower back. She felt a hand touch her elbow, then turned to see Stephane standing next to her. Marcia now had a full view of her nemesis. Mason was standing at the opposite side of the courtyard.

"How are you girls doing? I see you might need another drink," Stephane said to Marcia and Tiffany. He placed his own whiskey glass on the table.

"I definitely could use another drink," Marcia heard Tiffany say. Marcia glanced at her and saw that she was staring at Mason. Her eyes were so mesmerized by him that she didn't even look at Stephane when she spoke to him.

"Okay, I'll be right back, and then I'll take you to meet my future brother-in-law," Marcia heard Stephane say to them. Marcia didn't say a word; she just gave Stephane a weak nod. Her stomach turned, and she was nauseous at the thought of having to be cordial with Mason. She and Tiffany watched Stephane as he strolled to the bar to retrieve their drinks. Marcia lightly elbowed Tiffany in the side to stop her from eyeballing Mason.

"Stop staring at him. He's not going to do or say anything. There are too many people around," Marcia whispered to her.

"I don't even want to be in the same room as that bastard, or be near that asshole let alone shake his hand and pretend everything is fine," Tiffany said through between clenched teeth. Marcia noticed that Tiffany's hands were in tight balls.

"I know. We'll figure it out as we go along. I won't leave you alone. Just relax until we can make our exit," Marcia said, trying to reassure her.

The women admired the lights of Paris from their table while waiting for Stephane to return with their cocktails. They both turned their backs to Mason so he wouldn't spot them.

"Well, what brings you delicious ladies to Paris?" Marcia heard a man to her right say to them. Marcia and Tiffany whipped their heads in the direction of the voice. Mason was standing next to the table, leering at them with a smirk on his face.

* * *

115

Stephane was anxious to get back to Marcia. His foot tapped on the floor as he waited for the bartender to pour the wine. He didn't like leaving Marcia's side, especially since she didn't know the people at the reception. As he turned away from the bar, he noticed that Mason was talking to Marcia and Tiffany. *Someone must have introduced them to Mason while I was gone*, he thought. He walked down the hallway and headed back to the function area. After a few more strides, he was standing by Marcia. He placed the girls' drinks down on the table and touched Marcia's waist to let her know he was back, then left his hand on her hip.

"Here we go," Stephane said, turning his attention to his future brother-in-law. "Bonsoir, Mason, I see you met my dates. How are you?" he asked courteously as he shook Mason's hand.

"Good evening, Stephane. I'm doing just fine. Yes, I just met them, as a matter of fact, but I didn't know they were your dates," Mason answered as a devilish chuckle escaped him, and then he took a second look at the girls. Stephane frowned at him.

"Well, not both. Marcia is my girlfriend, and Tiffany is her friend. She's visiting her," Stephane said, pulling Marcia closer to his body and smiling down at her. *Why is she not responding to my touch or smile? She seems distracted and keeps looking away from me. Tiffany is chugging her drink down. She seems nervous too*, he thought.

"I'm positive you will enjoy your evening, Stephane. I should return to my fiancée, as I'm sure she's wondering where I am. Hopefully we shall see each other again soon. I'll talk to you later, Stephane," Mason said, then raised his glass and gulped down the rest of his bourbon. He placed the empty glass on the table and winked at the girls. *What a flirt!* Stephane thought, eyeing him. Mason turned around and walked over to join Etienne. Stephane refocused his energy on the girls. He saw that Tiffany was holding her clutch so hard that her knuckles were white. *How strange!* he thought.

"So, shall we find our table and have a seat? They will probably serve dinner soon," Stephane asked Marcia and Tiffany.

Marcia looked up at him, gave him a weak smile, and said, "Sure, that would be great."

He took her hand in his and led the way to one of the front tables. As he approached, he recognized a few friends who were already sitting down at the table, and he greeted them. It was a large table, so he decided to sit at the far end, away from his family, because he didn't want to make Marcia uncomfortable, as she didn't know them very well. Plus, several of Etienne's girlfriends were there, and she hadn't seen them in a while, so they probably preferred to sit near her. He and Marcia would have enough time with his family later in the evening. As he pulled out Marcia's chair, then Tiffany's, he said, "Here we are."

After the two girls chose their seats, he sat down next to Marcia and placed his right hand on her knee, which he always did for reassurance. He loved to touch her at all times.

"This is really nice. It's a lovely venue," Marcia said, not looking at him. Her attention was directed at the people in the hall, and her eyes kept scanning the room.

"Would you girls like another glass of wine?" Stephane asked them again. He noticed they had already finished their drinks.

"Yes, that sounds like a good idea. I'm kind of thirsty again. But just water for me." Marcia answered, turning to look at him for a moment before returning her gaze to the other guests that were sitting at the tables.

"All right. I'll be right back," Stephane said. Marcia didn't respond to him; she was whispering something to Tiffany that he couldn't hear. He stood up from the table and walked back to the bar. When he was halfway there, he glanced back at Marcia and Tiffany. They seemed to be having an intense conversation while watching the crowd, but they were not laughing or even smiling. He could see Tiffany's leg bouncing up and down under the table. She seemed agitated, and Marcia had a frustrated expression on her face. *I wonder what they are talking about that has them so high-strung. Marcia is usually calm and cheerful,* he thought. Shaking the thoughts away, he turned and continued to walk to the bar, then got in line at the counter. He waited as the bartenders filled other people's orders. Finally, a barmaid was standing in front of him.

"Bonsoir, what can I get you?" she asked politely.

"One glass of Chardonnay, a water, and a single malt whiskey on the rocks, please," Stephane said. He felt someone nudge him lightly in the arm, so he turned and saw that Mason had joined him at the bar. His back and elbows were leaning against the counter of the bar.

"So, tell me, Casanova, how long have you been dating Marcia, or is she a one night roll in the bed?" Mason asked, snickering.

Stephane licked his lips and took a long breath in, then released it slowly before answering him. "You are so obnoxious and rude when you are drinking."

Mason knew how to irritate him, and Stephane tried hard not to give in to his games. He cleared his throat before continuing.

"I met Marcia last month. We have been dating ever since," Stephane said, then gave him a fake smile. *Mason sure knows how to ruffle my feathers. Why do I let him? He has a foul mouth when he drinks,* Stephane thought. *One day I'm going to tell him to choose his words more carefully, but for the sake of my sister's feelings, I'll keep my mouth shut tonight.*

"Hmm, that's great news. Always fun, right?" Mason asked, laughing out loud.

"If you'll excuse me, Mason, I should get back to the girls. Catch you later," Stephane said. He grabbed the three drinks between his hands and left Mason standing alone at the bar. *Mason is drunk, as usual. I can't understand what my sister sees in that man*, he thought. He returned to the table where Marcia and Tiffany were waiting for him, then placed the three drinks in front of them.

"Here you go. One glass of white wine, and one glass of water for the most gorgeous woman in the room," he joked, taking his seat next to Marcia once again.

"Thank you," Marcia said, pushing her drink to the side. She pivoted her body in her seat so she was facing him. Taking both of his hands in hers, she looked him straight in the eye.

"Stephane, I'm so sorry, but Tiffany isn't feeling well. I'm going to grab a cab and take her home," Marcia said.

"Is she okay? What's the matter?" Stephane asked quietly. He leaned to the side to peek at Tiffany, who was staring at the bar area. *She does look a little pale, and there are beads of sweat on her temples. Maybe it's something she ate*, he thought.

"She'll be fine. Don't worry. I'll take care of her. You stay with your family and give me a call later," Marcia said.

"No, no, it's okay. I'll drive you home. Just give me a minute. I'll go tell Etienne I'm taking you home," Stephane told her. He started to stand, but she gripped his hand tightly, so he sat down again.

"Stephane, please. Etienne will be upset if you leave her engagement party to drive us back. I want you to stay and enjoy yourself. We will be fine," Marcia said.

She mouthed the word please, so he nodded his head. "All right, but I want you to text me when you get home, and I will stop by tonight before I return home," Stephane said, even though he didn't like it.

"Okay, thanks. Again, I'm sorry," Marcia said. Stephane nodded. Marcia then reached over and touched Tiffany's arm. They all stood up together.

"I'm so sorry you don't feel well, Tiffany. I hope you get better soon. I'll walk you out," Stephane said.

"I'm so sorry," he heard Tiffany say to both of them, then she bowed her head.

He led the way out of the reception area, and Marcia and Tiffany followed closely behind him. When they arrived outside of the hotel, the doorman flagged down a cab for them. Stephane opened the door, and Tiffany got in. He grabbed Marcia's waist and pulled her close to him before she could get in the vehicle.

"I'll miss you while you're away from me. Give me a call later and let me know how she's feeling, okay?" Stephane said, then kissed her on the lips before she departed. He watched the cab drive away, a feeling of emptiness consuming him, and then he turned on his heels and headed back inside the hotel to the engagement party.

Chapter 10

As they entered the apartment, Marcia noticed that Tiffany's hands were trembling, but some of the color had returned to her face. Not a word was spoken in the taxi on the short drive back to her home. They both were motionless, in a state of shock. Marcia had reached over to Tiffany in the cab and held her hand. Now there was an eerie silence as Marcia's mind tried to digest what she had just discovered: Mason was Stephane's sister's fiancé. *How am I going to deal with this problem?* she kept asking herself over and over, but no answers came to mind.

Marcia locked the door behind them, then threw her bag and keys on the kitchen counter. She went to join Tiffany, who was slumped on the sofa in the living room. They sat side by side, not uttering a word for what seemed a long time, but in reality, it was only a few minutes. They were both consumed in their own thoughts.

"Now what are we going to do? Are you going to tell Stephane about Mason, or are we just going to ignore what he does?" Tiffany asked, turning to look at Marcia.

Marcia shrugged and rubbed her hands together, unable to think straight. "I don't know. If I tell him, he will find out what I used to do for work, and then he'll leave me. He'll want to know how I know that Mason beats women for his own pleasure. What if Mason informs him about our former professions? Oh my God! I'll for sure lose Stephane," Marcia said to Tiffany as tears rolled down her cheeks.

Tiffany reached over and put her arm around Marcia's shoulder.

"Don't cry, Marcia. We will find a way to fix this without Stephane finding out. Mason will not win this battle. One way or another, we will expose him for who he is...an evil man," Tiffany said, trying to reassure Marcia.

"But how?" Marcia sobbed, tears causing her mascara to run down and stain her face. "I just found the love of my life, and now I might lose him because of this bastard. I must find an answer. Marcia said then she hid her face with her hands and sobbed.

"I'm determined to expose him, but what price will I pay if Stephane finds out I worked as an escort in the past?"

Tiffany hugged her, and Marcia knew she felt some of her pain.

"Come on! Dry your tears. Let's get out of these dresses and put something more comfortable on. Then we can have another glass of wine and figure out a solution together," Tiffany said, standing up.

She bent down and wiped Marcia's cheeks with her palms, then extended her hand to help Marcia get up. Marcia nodded at her friend, but she hesitated for a second before finally getting the courage to take Tiffany's hand and walk to the bedroom to change her clothes.

Twenty minutes later they were snuggled on the couch, a blanket wrapped around them both while they sipped on white wine.

"You know, Mason has as much to lose as you do. He is not stupid enough to expose you, because Etienne would not marry him. If she finds out he used escort services for his own pleasure, she won't forgive him, especially when she knows he beats women," Tiffany said, but it didn't make Marcia feel any better.

"Yes, maybe, but...what if Mason hurts Etienne the way he hurt you. Stephane will be furious that I never told him the truth. He might not forgive me, and he will leave me. In the end, I lose." Marcia contemplated the situation, and tears began flowing down her cheeks again as she thought of losing Stephane.

"Maybe I could trap him or threaten him. I could tell him that if he goes forward with the wedding, I'm going to tell Etienne about what he did to me. That way, you wouldn't be involved," Tiffany suggested, then sat upright on the edge of the sofa as she waited for an answer from Marcia.

"It might work, but how are we going to find him? I think he's staying at Stephane's parents' house for the party, but he's probably staying at one of the local hotels for this weekend, considering the festivities. I could discreetly ask Stephane by pretending I want to see Etienne. That might work and find out where he is. All I know is that I need to try to protect Etienne. Maybe if Stephane finds out about me, he will forgive me since I'm helping his sister," Marcia thought out loud while tapping her finger on her mouth. She smiled, then grabbed a tissue from her pocket and wiped the tears from her cheeks.

"That's brilliant! I think that will work. At least it's a start," Tiffany said.

Marcia nodded slowly, still unsure of their plan, and gulped down the last drops of her wine.

* * *

Stephane returned to his table in the reception area, a little disappointed that Marcia had left so abruptly. He sat down for the meal, keeping an eye on his phone as he waited to hear that Marcia had gotten home safely. Then he saw a small handbag on the table. It looked like Tiffany's, so he figured she must have forgotten it. He grabbed his phone from his pocket and texted Marcia to ask her about it. She replied and said that it was Tiffany's, so he offered to drop off the pocketbook after dinner. He inquired how Tiffany was feeling and Marcia told him she was much better. He already missed Marcia, and it was the perfect excuse to see her again later in the night.

The waitresses were picking up the last of the dessert plates when someone took a seat next to Stephane.

"How's it going, future brother-in-law?" he heard Mason mumble.

Stephane glanced over, closed his eyes momentarily, and balled his fists. *Oh hell, he's drunk again.* The red glassy eyes and slurred speech made it obvious that he had had too much to drink. He could barely sit up straight in his chair. Stephane pursed his lips tightly. He hated it when Mason drank that much. He became detestable and loud. Stephane watched as Mason placed his tumbler on the table, spilling half of it.

"Hey, buddy, how's it going? Why don't I drive you to your hotel? I think you had a little too much to drink. You wouldn't want Etienne to be upset with you during your engagement party, would you?" Stephane asked, trying to make sure Mason didn't embarrass his sister and family in front of their guests by making a fool of himself.

"No, no, I am just fine. I'm having a blast!" Mason replied in a mocking French accent as he picked up his drink and swallowed the last drop of whiskey. He pointed to his tumbler. "Well, I believe I need another one."

"Come on! I need to drop this purse off at my girlfriend's apartment; her friend forgot it. I'll have another drink with you at your hotel. What do you say?" Stephane asked in a calm voice, although his anger was building.

People were now looking at them, and Stephane could feel a headache coming. Mason tilted his head, smirked, and chuckled to himself, then nodded at Stephane.

"Okay, let's go," Mason said. Relief came over him that they were leaving. As Mason tried to stand up from his seat, his right hand grabbed the back of the chair for balance. "I'll just go tell mon amour that I'm leaving," he muttered as he pointed to Etienne at the other end of the room.

He took a step in her direction. Stephane didn't want Etienne to get upset, so he firmly grabbed Mason's arm to stop him and said, "That's okay. She's busy talking to her girlfriends. I'll text her in the car. Let's go."

Mason took one last glance over at Etienne, licked his lips, and nodded. Stephane picked up the handbag in one hand and held on to Mason's arm with the other. They discreetly walked out of the function as quickly as Mason could manage. At the valet station outside, Stephane dug his ticket out of his suit jacket and gave it to the parking attendant. They stood at the entrance of the hotel and waited for the young man to fetch the car. The cool, night breeze was refreshing, especially compared to Mason's alcoholic breath.

"So, tell me, what do you know about your lady friend? She's a beauty. Marcia...you said was her name?" Mason asked as the car approached the curb.

Stephane scowled at him and didn't answer. *Mason's had too much to drink. Don't bother answering him,* he thought. *Just keep your cool and take him home.* The valet brought his Bentley around, then jumped out of the driver's seat and ran to open the passenger door. Stephane escorted Mason to the passenger seat. He gave the young man a tip before hurrying around to the driver's side, starting the engine, and taking off through the streets of Paris.

"You should have a threesome with them. It might be fun. I'm just saying, before you ever get married, it's something to consider," Stephane heard Mason say, and then laughter echoed next to him.

He kept his eyes on the road, squeezing the steering wheel tightly, and tried to ignore the rude comments. By now his temples were throbbing even worse than before.

"I'm very content with one woman, thank you," Stephane managed to say under his breath.

"Don't knock it until you try it. You might enjoy it," Mason answered, snickering.

Stephane turned and glared at him, disgusted with his behavior, but he bit his tongue, choosing not to reply. He hated the way Mason acted when he was inebriated. His mouth was filthy, and he didn't care what came out of it. Mason disrespected everyone in his path, never having a single care for other people's feelings. Stephane wondered again why Etienne was thinking about marrying this man. The only reason Stephane tolerated Mason was because his sister loved him. She was blind to his derogatory conduct.

"So where are we going again? I thought we were going to see the girls? I could use another whiskey," Mason said as he slouched even lower in the passenger seat.

Stephane quickly glanced at Mason. "Like hell you're seeing the girls, and like hell you need another drink!" he muttered under his breath. "I'm just going to drop this clutch off at Marcia's, and then I'll take you to your hotel."

Finally, Stephane turned on Marcia's street and parked his vehicle in front of her apartment building. He grabbed the clutch, then noticed Mason reaching for the door handle. He immediately took a hold of his arm and said, "Why don't you stay here, close your eyes, and wait in the car? I'll be right back in a minute or two."

Mason let go of the handle, nodded, and sat back in his seat.

Stephane opened his door and walked to the intercom system at the front of the building. He pressed the button for Marcia's apartment, and her soft voice answered, "Who is it?"

"It's me, darling," Stephane said, and he heard the door buzz to let him in. He glanced over at Mason before entering the building and saw that he had fallen asleep. When he walked up to Marcia's apartment, she opened the door before he could knock. She stood in the doorway, waiting for him to take the last few steps to her. *She looks even more appetizing in sweats, with no makeup and her hair messed up*, he thought.

"Hi, you could have waited until morning to drop off her pocketbook," Marcia said as she took a step back to let him in.

He leaned forward and pulled her against his body, then kissed her passionately. "Hmm! I already missed you," he whispered in her ear as he inhaled the lavender scent of her hair. She giggled.

"I didn't just come by to drop it off. I also wanted to see if you were available for dinner tomorrow night at my place. I'll cook," he said as he pulled her even closer to him, rubbing the lower part of his body against her. As he slowly kissed the nape of her neck, he could feel an erection growing. *I wish I didn't have to drive Mason home. Maybe I could've stayed*, he thought.

"Well, I suppose I could. What's for dinner?" Marcia whispered. He felt her hand stroke his back.

"Me!" Stephane murmured in her ear.

She laughed, and her hand stopped on his chest, resting there. Gently pushing him away from her body, she looked up at him and smiled, tilting her head to the side. Out of the corner of his eye, Stephane saw Tiffany, who was watching them and grinning as she sat on the sofa in the living room.

"Sorry, I forgot you had company. Hi, Tiffany, I just came by to drop this off. Have a good night," Stephane said, a little abashed. He showed her the clutch in his hand, then passed it to Marcia.

Turning to Marcia, he continued, saying, "Seven o'clock, okay? I'll pick you up." He kissed her one more time on the mouth and exited the apartment. Marcia closed the door behind him, and he returned to his car, smiling from ear to ear.

* * *

The next day passed slowly. The girls stayed home and discussed how they were going to trap or expose Mason. Without one of them getting involved, they didn't have any concrete evidence of his fetish.

Marcia was in the bedroom getting ready for her date with Stephane, and Tiffany sat on the bed, leafed through a magazine, and watched as Marcia put on her makeup. Marcia was brushing her hair, but she suddenly stopped and stood motionless, brush in hand. She spun around to look at Tiffany, her eyes wide and her mouth open.

"Tiffany, why do you think Mason is marrying Etienne? Do you truly believe she's the right woman for him…or that he would give up his pleasures for her? No! Mason is marrying her because of her family's wealth. What if I bribed him to return to America and leave Etienne?" Marcia said excitedly, jumping up and down.

She threw the brush down on her bed and went to sit beside her friend. Tiffany didn't move; she just looked up at Marcia and listened. She put the magazine down next to her, her mouth opening and then closing, but a sound never came out.

"Well, what do you think? I truly don't believe he's in love with her. She is too innocent for him," Marcia said, waiting for Tiffany's response.

"It depends… How much do you think he would want? Or, more importantly, how much can we offer him?" Tiffany asked.

Marcia bit her lower lip as she tried to remember how much she had in investments.

"I'm willing to give him every penny I have in order to get him out of my life. I have a little over a million dollars saved up. What do you think?" Marcia asked.

"That's a lot of money. What guarantee do we have that he won't take the money, run, and then not keep his word? He might decide to stay after all. Then what?" Tiffany questioned.

"It's a chance I'm prepared to take in order to keep my secret and protect Etienne. I love Stephane with all of my heart, and I don't want to lose him. If I remember correctly, I heard something about how his construction company isn't as profitable as it used to be and that he was in financial troubles. My money might just bail him out, and then he wouldn't need Etienne's money. Maybe he'll just take it and leave," Marcia said enthusiastically.

"Okay, I'll help you. I'll give you five hundred thousand dollars more. That way, he might get greedy and agree to it. If he runs away with our money, I swear I'll kill him," Tiffany said.

Marcia eyes teared up at her best friend's thoughtfulness.

"I can't let you do that. This is my problem. You need your money," Marcia said.

"Sweetie, I have more than enough. I want you to have your love story, and I don't want to hear another word about it," Tiffany said, and then she reached over and hugged her.

"Someday I will pay back every penny, one way or another," Marcia said as she held her friend tightly and her eyes pooled.

"Okay, I'll ask Stephane where Etienne and Mason are staying so we can set up a meeting with the bastard, and then we'll will go from there," Marcia said.

As she spoke, she heard the apartment bell ring, and a wide smile appeared on her face.

"That must be Stephane! I'll return after dinner. I shouldn't be too late," Marcia said as she sprung to her feet and raced to meet him at the door. After grabbing her shawl from the edge of the bed, she left the room. As always, she opened the door before he could get there, watching as he walked toward her in the hallway.

"You look beautiful, as always. Ready?" Stephane asked, then kissed her on the lips.

"Yes, all set," Marcia said, taking his hand in hers.

After dinner Marcia and Stephane were sitting on his balcony, sipping expressos and watching the people down below on the street.

"I was wondering, where are Etienne and Mason staying in town? I wanted to give Etienne a call. Maybe we could have lunch while she's in Paris," Marcia said casually.

"That's a great idea! I'm sure she would love it. They are staying at The Four Seasons Hotel on George V Avenue," Stephane answered as he placed his arm around her shoulder.

"I'll give her a call tomorrow. By the way, dinner was fabulous. I didn't know you were such a wonderful chef," Marcia teased as she nestled closer to him in her seat.

"Well, now you have to pay for your dinner," Stephane said.

He wrapped his arms tighter around her and kissed her. Their tongues danced. She didn't resist and kissed him back eagerly. She had missed him. The lust enveloped her body, and she closed her eyes as she pressed her erect nipples against his chest. Pulling away slightly, her hand played with his dark hair while she became hypnotized by the blue eyes staring down at her. She held on to him like it was her last night. Suddenly she heard him whisper, "Je t'aime," just before his mouth crashed on hers again.

Chapter 11

Marcia could hear birds chirping outside through the open window in Stephane's bedroom. She could smell the sweat of their lovemaking on her body and on her pillow, where her head rested. She didn't move, nor did she open her eyes. Warm breath could be felt as he breathed shallowly against her neck, and a strong hand cupped her right breast. *Boy, I wish this moment would never end and that it could stay like this forever*, she thought.

Suddenly she remembered what Stephane had whispered to her the previous night. *Did I hear him say he loves me, or did I imagine those words?* She had longed to hear those words from a man for such a long time. *Yes, I am sure he said it. He loves me. What a fool I am! Why didn't I tell him I love him too?* She slowly turned her body so she could see his face. He stirred in his sleep; however, he didn't wake. She stared at him for a few minutes as he slept soundly, memorizing every little part of his face, from his curved eyebrows to his perfect lips to the second day shadow that she loved so much.

She then remembered that she had not planned to stay the night at Stephane's place. Tiffany would be wondering where she was, as

Marcia had told her she would be back after dinner. *I'm sure she is just fine anyway. I'll return to the apartment soon. Tiffany is a big girl. She can take care of herself for one evening.* She felt a pang of guilt for leaving Tiffany alone, but she forgot about it as soon as Stephane's arm dragged her closer to his body.

"Bonjour, mon amour," his sexy voice whispered, but he didn't open his eyes to look at her.

"Bonjour, did you sleep well?" Marcia asked, leaning forward and lightly kissing him on the mouth.

Just the slight contact of his lips touching hers made her shiver with desire, but she knew she had to get home.

"When you are by my side, I always sleep like a baby," Stephane answered, then opened his eyes and smiled at her.

Marcia giggled at him as he held her tighter, his hand slipping down her belly and toward her legs. She could feel his erection pressing against her body.

"You know...you shouldn't..." Marcia started to protest, but she couldn't resist the urge that was building inside her. She moaned and closed her eyes to relish in the sensation. *One more hour, then I'll return home*, she thought. Straddling his body, she began to satisfy the hunger that had developed in her core during the last minute.

"I'll pick you and Tiffany up around seven o'clock for dinner. I will miss you deeply," Stephane said as they sat in his car in front of her apartment building. Her lips brushed his one last time, and then she pulled away, reaching for the handle of the door so she could get out and go meet up with Tiffany. She was so late.

"Aurevoir, see you this evening. Don't miss me too much." Marcia joked while laughing.

She opened the door and removed herself from his grip by placing his hand on the wheel.

"Okay, okay, we will finish this kiss when I see you again," Stephane said as she hopped out of the car and stepped out on the sidewalk.

She pushed the door shut and blew him a kiss. Opening the red door to the courtyard, she entered and hurried to her apartment, taking long strides. She turned the key in the lock of the door and heard the click of the clasp.

"Tiffany, I'm home. I'm so sorry I'm so late. I know I was supposed to be come home last night, but you know..." Suddenly her pocketbook dropped from her hand. Her legs felt weak, and her eyes opened wide. She quickly raised her hand to her mouth in shock, inhaling deeply. Her breathing stopped for a moment as her eyes scanned the room in horror. *Where's Tiffany?* That was all she could think of. The living area looked like a tornado had gone through it. The lamp was broken on the floor, the pictures were crooked on the walls, and the chair had been tipped over. A cold sweat surfaced on her back as she tried to refocus her energy and find Tiffany. She exhaled, then slowly took a few steps forward, examining the area, but Tiffany was nowhere to be seen in the living room or kitchen.

"Tiffany, where are you? Tiffany?" Marcia screamed as she went in the direction of the bedroom. She ran up the stairs, taking them two at a time. Slowing her pace, she approached the bedroom door, but stopped immediately, afraid of what was on the other side. It was ajar. She swallowed hard. Her throat was dry, and tears were pooling in her eyes. She pressed her ear against the door and listened for any unusual noises, but everything was quiet.

She reached out with a trembling hand and pushed the door with her fingertips, anticipating the worst. As the door swung open, she glanced around the room and saw Tiffany lying on the floor, her hair disheveled, dried blood caked on her upper lip. Her left eye was swollen and blue. Marcia gasped, and her adrenaline spiked. *Oh my God! What happened, Tiffany? Are you okay?* her mind screamed, but her body stood stationary. She snapped out of it and ran to kneel near her, her hand quivering as she pushed the hair from her face. Tiffany stirred. *Thank God! She's alive!*

"Tiffany, sweetie, I'm so sorry. What happened? Who did this? Let me help you get on the bed," Marcia said.

She placed her arm around Tiffany's shoulders and lifted her into a sitting position, carefully setting on edge of the bed. Tiffany whimpered as she touched her head with her hand.

"I'm...I'll be all right," Tiffany answered, dazed. She looked around the room, trying to focus.

"Who did this? Hold on, I'm calling the police, and then I'll call an ambulance so I can take you to the hospital," Marcia said as she reached for her phone in the back pocket of her pants. She felt a hand grip her on her arm, so she looked down. Tiffany was shaking her head at her.

"No...no, I'll be fine," Tiffany said. "Just help me get on the bed," Marcia wrapped her arms around her waist and helped her up.

Tiffany grimaced while grabbing her side, then relaxed, resting her head against the pillow. Marcia sat next to her and watched as Tiffany closed her eyes.

"You need to see a doctor. Please, at least let me call someone. Who did this, Tiffany? Do you know?" Marcia questioned, but Tiffany didn't answer. "I'll be right back. Stay put."

Marcia ran to the bathroom, grabbed a towel, and turned the cold water on, wetting the towel. She grabbed a cup from the counter and filled it with water, then marched back to sit next to her friend. After tenderly wiping the blood off of Tiffany's face, she brought the cup to Tiffany's mouth so she could take a sip of water. Tears began to fall down Tiffany's face.

"He did it again. I thought I was done with all of this crap, but I suppose I will never be. I've been so careful all of these years. It was Mason," Tiffany whispered, then began to sob.

"What? How? Oh no! Tiffany, I'm so sorry. I should never have left you alone. If I hadn't gone out..." Marcia trailed off, not believing what she had heard. She hugged her friend. Anger raged inside of her, and she clenched her teeth and balled her fists. "How did he find us? Tell me what that bastard did."

"It wasn't your fault. If you had been here, he would have hurt you too. Last night, about half an hour after you left, the doorbell rang. I thought you had forgotten your keys or something. I didn't ask who it was. Stupid me, right? I buzzed the courtyard door to let you in, then unlocked the apartment door. When I opened the door, he pushed his way inside. I tried to stop him but..." Tiffany cried. Marcia hugged her again. "He was too strong. I couldn't stop him from..." Tiffany wept uncontrollably. Tears streamed down her face. *How could this happen to her again? I should have been home.*

"Fucking bastard! I'm going to kill him. I'm calling the police," Marcia said as fury invaded her body.

"No, Marcia, you can't. It will be my word against his. He'll say I let him in or that I seduced him. You know how it goes with our line of work. I'll be okay. I've been there before. You know that. I'll survive, and you have Stephane to think about," Tiffany said.

The reality sunk in for Marcia. *Stephane...what would I tell him? He would never understand. Oh dear Lord!* She had finally found a man to love, but she would lose him if he ever discovered the truth. *What am I going to do?* She had to choose between her best friend and her man.

"Very well, I won't do anything, but one day I will find a way to make him pay for what he did to you," Marcia said as she embraced Tiffany again.

An hour later Marcia heard the whole story from Tiffany—how Mason had found out where they lived when Stephane had dropped off Tiffany's handbag, how he had pushed his way into their place, how Tiffany had tried to fight back. But the more she had resisted, the worse it had made the situation. It had only infuriated him more, and he had taken advantage of poor Tiffany.

Later, when Tiffany went to take a hot shower, the first thing Marcia did was call Stephane. She hated to lie to him, but she had no choice. She dialed his number. She waited as his phone rang once, twice, and then she heard his voice.

"Bonjour. Stephane LaRoche," he answered.

"Bonjour, Stephane. It's Marcia. How are you?" Marcia asked as she paced back in forth in the living room.

"I'm just fine. I can't wait to see you. I was just about to leave the office and return home."

"I'm not going to be able to meet you this evening. Tiffany is sick with the flu, and I don't want to leave her alone, so I'm going to have to cancel our plans. I'm so sorry," Marcia said, hoping he wouldn't hear how nervous she was.

"I'm so sorry to hear that. I am disappointed, but it can't be helped. I will miss you. Is there anything I can do?"

Maria sighed with relief when she realized he wasn't angry.

"I will miss you too. No, I think she just needs to rest. I will talk to you tomorrow. Aurevoir."

"Okay, I'll see you tomorrow. Aurevoir."

Marcia hung up before he could ask any more questions.

Tiffany and Marcia sat huddled together on the sofa in the living room for hours. They both had bloodshot eyes from crying, and empty teacups sat beside them on the coffee table. Marcia's heart ached so much for Tiffany, and she was sick to her stomach. She knew that deep down she had enough rage inside of her to kill the son of a bitch for what he had done to her best friend. Both women sat in silence, consumed with their own thoughts. Marcia was brought back from her daze when Tiffany said, "I'm so sorry, Marcia, but I'm going to return to the United States as soon as I can. I can't stay here."

Marcia felt another tear roll down her cheek. She felt like someone was stabbing her in the heart.

"I wish you would stay. We could move. We could..." Marcia trailed off, knowing she wouldn't be able to convince her to stay.

Tiffany bowed her head and shook it from side to side while sobbing. "I'm too terrified to stay. I need to be in my surroundings. I want to be home."

"I know, baby. I'm so sorry." Marcia wrapped her arms around her friend. *That bastard! I swear I'm going to make it my mission to ruin his life*, she thought. After pulling away from the embrace, she wiped the tears off Tiffany's bruised face, then nodded at her. Tears rolled down her cheeks. "I understand. It's okay. You need to at least get a good night's sleep so you can travel. Let's go to bed. I'll help you gather your things and pack tomorrow." She said with a heavy heart.

Tiffany nodded in agreement, and Marcia took her hand as they walked upstairs to her bedroom.

The next day Marcia stood by the boarding security gate and watched as Tiffany walked down the roped area to her gate. Tiffany waved one last time, mouthed "I love you," and then disappeared behind the wall. Marcia bowed her head as tears pooled her eyes behind her sunglasses. *How could this happen to Tiffany again? I should have been with her to protect her. She's the strong one, the one who always knows the solution to any problem. She will prevail with time,* she thought. *Tiffany has been so cautious to avoid that evil man. She warned all of the girls at work about Mason, urging them to never take him as a client. Why did this have to happen to her?*

Marcia inhaled deeply, then turned slowly and sauntered toward the exit. With every step she took, fury invaded her being. She stood straighter, held her head higher, and clenched her fists tightly. "I will have my revenge. You will never hurt anyone else again. I will find a way to bring you down, even if it's the last thing I ever do, even if I lose Stephane along the way," she whispered under her breath.

Marcia lay in a hot tub of water, her eyes closed, her head resting on the rim of the tub. She was trying to relax and figure out what to do about Mason when she heard a ping from her phone. She opened her eyes, sat up and reached over to grab it, and then looked at the message. Can't wait to see you at seven. On my way soon.

Shit! I completely forgot that Stephane was coming, she thought.

Earlier in the day, she had lied to Stephane and told him that Tiffany had to leave unexpectedly so she could go back home and deal with a death in her family. He had been completely sympathetic and had offered to take her to dinner.

She glanced at the time on her phone and saw that it was ten after six. It would be rude to cancel two days in a row, but she didn't want to see him tonight; she was too exhausted. As she was starting to text a cancellation, another message came through from him.

I invited my sister and Mason to join us for dinner. I hope you don't mind.

A mental image flashed before her of Mason grinning at her in his secret glory as they sat at the table at dinner. A rush of anger flared up, and she could feel her heart racing. She despised him. *How can I sit across from that bastard when I know what he has done to Tiffany?* All she wanted to do was punch the man until he was black and blue. She wanted him to suffer for what he had done to Tiffany, give him a dose of his own medicine.

Suddenly she had a revelation, and she knew how she could destroy him. Laughing out loud, she texted Stephane back. **No problem. That's a great idea. See you soon!**

Later, after taking a shower, she jumped out of the tub, dried off, and ran to her closet. She grabbed a short, low-cut Chanel dress and her six-inch black Prada heels, then threw them on the bed and began to put makeup on and dry her hair. Forty-five minutes later she stood in front of the mirror admiring her masterpiece. She realized that Stephane might not like how she looked, as she was dressed like she would have dressed for a call at her old job, but she knew Mason would appreciate it. Her breasts were showing; her bare legs were gleaming; her curly hair was pinned up, only a few strands falling against her face; and she had on full face of makeup and bright red lipstick.

The doorbell rang just as she was coming down the courtyard steps. She stopped for a second in front of the door, preparing herself. Tonight she was not Marcia; she was Catherine, the exotic woman that men spent money on and hired for evenings. Taking a deep breath, she put a smile on her face. She was ready for anything that Mason brought to the table.

"Wow! Maybe we should just stay in and not go to dinner," Stephane said as his eyes widened.

He looked her over from head to toe, then placed his hands on her hips and pulled her close to him. When he kissed her on the neck, she laughed and gently pushed him away.

"No, we should go meet Etienne and Mason. We don't want to be late," Marcia said in a low, sexy tone.

He nodded, giving in, and escorted her out to his car. After she got in, she watched as he strapped his seatbelt in. He looked up at her again and smiled.

"You look amazing. Are you sure you don't want to stay in tonight? Last chance..." he said, teasing her.

She knew that he was hoping she would change her mind, but tonight she had other plans.

"Not tonight, sweetie," she said, then stared straight ahead and avoided his eyes. This evening, she was on her own personal mission.

* * *

Stephane stood at the door, his mouth falling open as he looked at Marcia. She didn't look like the simple woman he had been dating, the lady he had fallen in love with, but she did look extremely flamboyant. He thought she was beautiful, but would have preferred if she hadn't worn such a revealing dress. Because of the cut of the front of her dress, which went all the way down to her waist, it was easy for him to eye her firm breasts. He noticed the fake eyelashes, the makeup, and the heels, and the scent of vanilla spice could be smelled when he kissed her. It drove him wild, and an erection had started growing the minute he saw her.

He drove to the Four Seasons Hotel George V, where the three Michelin star restaurant Le Cinq was located. After he parked in front of the hotel, he got out of the car and gave the valet fifty euros to keep his Bentley by the curb. Stephane glanced over to the other side of the car just as another valet opened Marcia's door. She gracefully exited the car, smiled at the young man—who seemed captivated by her—and said, "Thank you!"

She's so beautiful. I'm so lucky that she's mine, Stephane thought. He observed her as she walked to the front entrance and waited for him. Her hips sensually moved from side to side, her head held high. He joined her at the entrance, placing his hand on her lower back so he could claim ownership before they entered the restaurant.

"All set?" he asked casually, and she nodded confidently, then gave him a smile that took his breath away. She didn't wait for him; instead, she immediately took a step toward the entryway. He noticed that the slit in her dress displayed her thigh as she walked. As she moved through the lobby of the elegant hotel, he followed closely behind her.

The Four Seasons was one of the most stunning hotels in Paris. There were antique gold-colored benches made of velvet. The marble floors and pillars glistened, and the crystal chandeliers were shimmering. The staff was dressed in gold and black, smiling at Stephane and Marcia as they entered the restaurant. Marcia slowed down her pace as they approached the entrance of Le Cinq, where the maître d'hôtel was waiting to receive them.

"Good evening, how may I help you?" the young woman asked them.

"Bonsoir, we have seven o'clock reservations under the name LaRoche." Stephane answered.

They waited patiently as she looked up his name on the computer, then picked up the menus and a wine list.

"Yes, Monsieur LaRoche, if you would follow me...right this way," she answered, then headed inside the restaurant.

The tables were decorated with ornate white tablecloths and gray and gold chinaware, embellished with crystal glasses. A pianist played soft music by the side of the bar. Stephane spotted his sister and her fiancée, who were waiting for them by one of the grand windows in the back area of the dining room. Etienne smiled and waved her hand when she saw them approaching the table, and Mason stood up to greet them.

"Bonsoir, sorry we are late. Have you been waiting long?" Stephane asked as he shook Mason's hand, then leaned down to kiss his sister's cheek.

"Not at all. We just ordered a drink while waiting for you. How are you this evening, Marcia? Please, have a seat." Etienne replied, a smile lighting up her face.

"I'm very well, thank you," Marcia said, and then she leaned toward Mason, smiled, and kissed his cheek. She then sat next to Mason, crossed her leg in his direction, and placed her small bag on the table.

Stephane took the seat next to his sister. *Weird! Marcia didn't even sit near Etienne. I thought she wanted to spend more time with her,* he thought.

"What would you like to drink?" Mason asked, directing his gaze toward Marcia.

Stephane noticed that Mason was glancing at her breasts while he talked to her, and he glared at him, but didn't say anything.

Marcia lightly rested her hand on Mason's arm and said, "I'll have what you're having."

"Don Perignon, it is! What about you, Stephane?" Mason asked, his eyes locked on Marcia. He smirked at her until Etienne placed her hand on his knee, trying to redirect his attention.

As the evening progressed, Stephane noticed that Marcia was paying a lot of attention to Mason. She would lean close to him every time he spoke and whisper things to him—things Stephane couldn't hear. He was annoyed at her behavior, but he didn't say anything, trying to keep his cool. She was being more talkative than usual with Mason. Her hands were always touching his hand or his knee as she spoke. Etienne seemed to be trying her best not to show her disgust, but her frown gave it away.

Stephane put his hand on Marcia's knee under the table and squeezed it gently, trying to get Marcia to stop, but she just kept on going. She was testing his patience; he was embarrassed by her conduct as well as the lack of respect she was showing his sister and him. The worst part was that Mason didn't seem to mind the attention.

"You have to taste this dessert. It melts in your mouth," Marcia said seductively to Mason, then licked her lips.

Stephane clenched his teeth. He could feel the heat rise to his face as he watched Marcia take her spoon, scoop up a bite of her chocolate soufflé, and then put it in Mason's mouth, all while giggling with him. Then he saw her brush her leg against Mason's. That was the last straw. It was as if he wasn't even present, worst of all was the disregard of his sister. He had had enough of this display between Mason and Marcia.

He glanced at his sister, who seemed to be stunned by Marcia's actions. She was glaring at both of them, and he could see that she was almost ready to burst. Her lips were pursed tightly as she tried to keep her fiancée from making a fool of himself in public, to no avail.

She looked away, trying to pretend it didn't bother her, but Stephane knew better. She was mortified and hurt.

Stephane grabbed his napkin and threw it on the table, then stood up.

"Thank you for a nice dinner, but I think it's time for us to leave. Let's go, Marcia," he said sternly, then took her free hand in his and pulled it, trying to direct her attention away from Mason.

She looked up at him briefly, but she didn't budge. By the scowl she gave him, he could tell she was irritated.

"Don't leave just yet. Let's have another drink...one for the road," Stephane heard Mason say nonchalantly.

He could see that Mason was enjoying the situation and that he had had too much to drink. He was trying to have his way, which was testing Stephane's self-control.

"It's late, and time to leave...*now*. Thank you for dinner," Stephane said as calmly as he could.

He picked up Marcia's clutch and handed it to her, and she took it from him without looking his way.

"Yes, I suppose it's time to leave. Thank you for a pleasurable evening," Marcia said to Mason as she stood up slowly.

She leaned forward, giving Mason one last look at her breasts, all the while paying no attention to Stephane or his sister. She turned away and began walking toward the exit, and Stephane followed closely behind her.

He watched as her hips swayed, her hair bouncing as she strutted back to the entrance of the hotel. He glanced back briefly at the table and saw that Mason was smirking at Marcia and licking his lips as he watched her every move. Disgusted and speechless, Stephane quickened his pace, all the while trying to contain the anger and embarrassment that was building inside.

How could she humiliate me like that in front of my sister? Her hands were pawing all over Mason all night long. It was as if I wasn't even there. What has gotten into her? She barely talked to anyone but him. Why? She'd better have one hell of an explanation! But there's really nothing that could justify her actions, he thought.

He was two steps behind her, watching as she walked with her chest sticking out and her head held high. She strolled toward the exit, completely unconcerned. Heads of other patrons turned to admire her, but her eyes were focused on the entrance of the lobby.

Stephane didn't utter a word. He reached in his pocket, took out his ticket, and passed it to the valet. He clamped his teeth together as he pondered on the evening events. *Why?* That was the only question that kept coming to mind.

He watched as the valet drove his vehicle to the front of the hotel and opened Marcia's door, then passed him an extra ten euros for his services. In the car he closed his door, placed his hands on the steering wheel, and sat motionlessly in his seat. Because he didn't want to blow up at Marcia, he kept looking straight ahead, for once keeping his eyes on the road. He drove away from Le Cinq restaurant in silence, trying to understand what had happened at dinner—what had happened with the woman he loved so much.

Chapter 12

Marcia's heart broke as she sat with her hands on her knees on the ride home. She didn't dare even peek at Stephane, knowing she had hurt him and that he was probably furious at her, that he must've been so embarrassed by her behavior. The silence was deadly, unbearable, but she held her head high, refusing to let her emotions show or take over. Not one word had been uttered from Stephane since he had thrown his napkin on the table, and she knew deep down how irritated and confused he had to be. She had seen the expression of disgust he had given her at the table, but it was her mission to destroy Mason. She couldn't think about anyone one's feelings, not even her own. It was her responsibility to get close to the bastard so she could break up his marriage and expose how despicable he was.

Turning her head toward the window, she watched the pedestrians walk down the street, the street signs passing her by. Finally, she could no longer stand the silence.

"How about a little music?" Marcia said as cheerfully as she could, reaching for the knob on the radio.

"Leave it alone! I don't feel like listening to music at this moment," he responded in an angry, flat tone.

She pulled her hand back in silence and sat back in her seat, waiting for him to explode at her. The muscles in his jaw tightened, and he exhaled loudly. Finally, he pulled up to the curb, parking the car in front of her apartment, and shut the ignition off. She glanced his way, but he was looking forward, staring into the distance. His grip on the wheel tightened as she stared at him and waited for him to speak.

"Goodnight," Stephane said quietly, not even glancing her way.

"Can I get a kiss before you leave?" Marcia whispered, trying to smooth things over a bit.

He turned toward her, his scowl piercing her heart, and she was sorry she had asked.

"You don't deserve a kiss after the way you behaved this evening. What the hell was the matter with you? You embarrassed me in front of my sister. You were all over her fiancée, of all people, and now you want a kiss?" he spit out at her.

What did you expect after the way you conducted yourself tonight? Did you think he was just going to forgive you that easily and let it pass? she thought. She bowed her head without a word. As she couldn't tell him what her plan was, she just had to sit there and take his wrath. Tears filled her eyes, but she blinked them away, knowing she had to be strong and selfish if this plan of hers was going to work.

"I'm sorry," she whispered, then leaned over to kiss him on the cheek.

He backed away from her embrace, turning his head away, and she closed her eyes momentarily, the pain piercing her heart. She knew she had to get used to it and ignore that feeling. Grabbing the handle of the door, she opened it and placed her feet on the ground, ready to exit, and then she heard Stephane say, "Wait!"

She didn't turn around, instead waiting for him to speak.

"I'll call you tomorrow," he said quietly.

"Goodnight," she answered, stepping out of the vehicle and shutting the door.

He avoided her gaze as she passed in front of the vehicle, and she stood motionlessly on the side of the curb, watching him drive away. Walking to her front door, she opened it and entered her apartment. As soon as the door closed behind her, tears pooled in her eyes, then rolled down her cheeks. She didn't want to hurt Stephane, she loved him so much. He was the only man she had ever love this deeply, but she had no choice she couldn't let his sister marry that bastard. Mason was evil and someone had to stop him. She had to expose him for who he was before he injured Etienne with his fetish or worst kill her.

After wiping her tears, she unzipped her dress as she walked up to her bedroom on the second floor, then threw her dress on the chair next to her bed.

If all of this meant she had to lose Stephane, then so be it. She knew what she needed to do, and she was determined to win. This evening she had dangled the bait in front of Mason, and it was clear that he wanted her. He would come to her soon. She had to be prepared for whatever happened.

The next morning Marcia woke at the break of dawn. She had had a restless night, waking up several times to listen for any sounds in her apartment. Rubbing the back of her neck, she tried to alleviate the soreness. She slipped her hand under the pillow next to her and brought it to her face. Stephane's scent was still on the pillowcase. She already missed him.

Stop it! You can't go down that road. You need to expose Mason. You need to be strong. Think! What is your next move? You know bribing him won't justify what he did or satisfy you. You need to be wise so that he won't catch on to your ruse or hurt you, she told herself. *I might have to give him a call; otherwise, how am I going to meet up with him? I'm sure I won't be invited to dinner very soon, especially not after yesterday evening's disaster or should I say success,"* she pondered.

She remembered that Mason had said during the previous evening that he liked to go to cafés close to his hotel so he could get an espresso in the mornings.

That's it, she thought.

She sat up in bed, thinking. *I could go find Mason and have coffee with him, or I could try to explain the situation to Stephane. Would he believe me if I told him the truth, or would he loathe me when he found out what I used to do?* She was torn.

"You can't think of Stephane's feelings," she said out loud.

After shoving the blanket off of her, she jumped out of bed and marched directly to the bathroom, turning the water on in the shower.

Within an hour she had pulled on a pair of ripped Louis Vuitton blue jeans and a light blue Gucci sweater that accentuated the curves of her breasts. She applied blush on her cheeks and a little lip gloss on her perfect lips, then picked up a bottle of her Givenchy perfume and sprayed some on. After slipping on a pair of loafers that were by her bed, she quickly brushed her hair, leaving it a bit messy. She ran down the stairs and went to her kitchen, grabbing her bag and an apple, and then she headed out the door.

Her focus was on Mason and getting to his hotel as she walked the streets with a brisk pace. Finally, she could see the hotel up ahead, only a couple of blocks. Slowing her stride, she scanned the street for a place to sit while she waited for Mason to exit. She spotted a bench under a tree across the street, not too far from the entrance of the hotel.

That's a perfect spot to spy on someone, she thought.

She made her way over there and sat down. When she glanced at her watch, she saw that it was ten till seven o'clock. After crossing her legs, she retrieved her apple and a pair of dark sunglasses from her bag. She bit into her apple, all the while keeping her eyes glued to the entrance. Minutes passed slowly, and she looked at her watch again. It was seven-thirty.

So many people have exited the hotel. Maybe I missed him. Or maybe he decided not to go out this morning, she thought.

A few minutes later she sat up straight as she noticed him coming out the revolving doors. He wore a pair of crisp black trousers, a polo shirt, and a light jacket. She couldn't move, her eyes following his every step. He walked with long strides toward the small café at the corner of the block, his hands deep in the pockets of his jacket. She observed him as he sat down at one of the small, round tables facing the street.

She stood up, her heart beginning to throb in her chest, her legs turning to jelly at the thought of having to sit by his side. *Don't panic! Stay the course*, she told herself. Raising her chin up, she took her first step forward. Her strut was smooth and calculated as her hips moved, her hair blowing away from her face. When she was about thirty feet from him, he looked up from his coffee and she tilted her head a bit and smiled at him. She stopped right in front of his table and gracefully took her shades off, then brushed her hair over her shoulder and sexually bit the corner of her lower lip.

"Well, bonjour, Mason. Nice to see you again so soon," she said cheerfully.

He rose from his chair to greet her, leaning forward to kiss her on the cheek. Just the simple touch of his mouth made her skin crawl, but she continued smiling.

"Bonjour, what are you doing in this area of town? Please join me for an early morning espresso," he said as he out pulled the chair next to him so she could sit down.

"Thank you. I love exploring the city by foot of the early mornings," she said in a low tone.

She sat down and crossed her legs, then consciously placed her right hand next to his so they would touch briefly. Mason raised his hand to get the waiter's attention, directing him to their table.

"Two more espressos, please," Mason said as he pointed to his empty cup.

His divided attention returned to Marcia, and he cupped one of her hands. His clammy hands on hers made her stomach turn, but she didn't move them. She just kept smiling at him.

"I'm delighted to have company this morning. What brings you this way?" Mason asked her as he licked his upper lip.

Disgusting! she thought, gently pulling her hand away and placing both hands on her knees.

"Oh, I'm usually up very early, and I love to walk around town, as I said. It relaxes me, and I get to find treasures along the way…like this beautiful café we are sitting at, for instance," she replied. The waiter arrived with their beverages and placed them down in front of them before walking away. "Where is Etienne this morning? She must be so busy with the wedding arrangements."

She took a sip of her espresso, trying to soothe her parched throat. Out of the corner of her eye, she noticed that he was watching her every move, just like a predator waiting to pounce on his prey.

"As I told you yesterday evening, she prefers to sleep in. I, on the other hand, prefer to get up early in the morning. Then I have more time to do as I please, like having coffee with you," Mason said, then grinned her way.

"Hmm, I understand completely," Marcia replied, giggling softly.

He seemed to like her response, as he leaned forward until he was only inches from her ear and whispered, "If you'd like, we could always meet in the early morning hours. I'm always free for a little extra loving, if you know what I mean."

He chuckled, and a nauseating feeling swept through her. She closed her eyes and swallowed hard. The thought of being with him made her want to throw up. His hand began to slowly stroke her thigh, and she immediately placed her hand over his to stop it from going any farther. She leaned toward him, making sure that he could smell her perfume and see the curves of her bosom.

"Well, you do understand that we would have to keep this private and that there would have to be the guarantee of a gift, right?" she asked in a flirty tone, knowing she had him hooked.

"Yes, I understand. So..." he said with a devilish smirk, his eyes dancing.

She waited a moment, not saying a word, and then picked up her cup and gulped down the last drop. Pushing her chair back, she immediately stood up.

"Thank you for the drink. Maybe we will see each other soon. I should be home in a bit, in an hour or so," she said, smiling.

He looked up at her, a surprised look on his face. His mouth opened, but no words came out. She turned on her heels and walked down the street, leaving him by himself at the café. Barely able to catch her breath, she struggled to keep her pace. She had set her trap, and he had fallen for it. Now all she needed to do was fine-tune it. As she approached her apartment, she quickened her pace, knowing he would come by soon. Her hands were shaking as she opened the door of her home. She closed the door behind her and took a deep breath as she tried to calm herself.

She needed to call Stephane right away and arrange for him to come see her at the precise moment when Mason was in her apartment; otherwise... Deep down she knew what kind of man he was. He would raise his hand against her, just as he had with Tiffany, if she didn't perform or if she refused his advances. Her heartbeat quickened at the thought, and a chill ran down her back.

Figuring he would show up early, she raced to the phone and dialed Stephane's number. Her grip tightened on the phone as she heard it ring once, twice, three times. No answer. She hadn't anticipated that he wouldn't be home to answer her call. *It's early in the morning. Where could he be?* She dialed his cell, but there was no answer there either.

A rush of adrenaline came over her, and heat rushed to her head. She couldn't breathe. *Don't panic just yet!* she thought. Closing her eyes, she listened as his voicemail came on.

"Stephane, it's me. I'm sorry about last night. Could you come over so we can talk? Please call me back," she pleaded, then hung up the phone.

He must be in the shower or something. Calm down. You can call him back. You have time, she thought. *But what if he's mad and doesn't want to talk to me because of last night?* Her plan was falling apart. She should have planned this rendezvous with Mason more carefully. Minutes ticked away as she paced the living room.

She heard a soft knock at the door, and then a man's voice said, "Marcia? It's me. Let me in."

Her head whipped toward the door at the sound of Mason's voice. He must have followed her home. She stared at the door, frozen with fear, then covered her mouth to keep her screams from escaping. She took a step backward. The doorknob began to turn, and then the door slid open slowly. She had forgotten to lock it, and now she was trapped. Her plan was not going to work. She could feel her chest tightening, so she took a deep breath, trying to catch her breath. Her whole body was shaking. As his figure entered the room, she straightened her back and held her head high, preparing herself to face anything.

* * *

Stephane reached over and turned the alarm clock off when it rang at seven o'clock that morning.

"Damn!" he said out loud.

A half-empty bottle of whiskey was on the side table next to his bed. He closed his eyes again, his temples pounding with pain from not having slept most of the night. His eyes opened slightly, but the light from the morning sun coming through the window hurt his eyes. *Why is it so bright?* he thought, squinting. He turned to his other side to avoid the brightness.

He didn't feel like getting up to go to work. All he had on his mind was Marcia, and he couldn't concentrate on anything else. Questions kept haunting him. *What was going on with Marcia? Why was she all over Mason last night? How could she humiliate me like that, especially in front of my sister? What did I do to make her act that way?* No answers seemed to come to him. He shook his head, not moving a muscle for a few more minutes.

I love this woman with all of my heart. I don't want to lose her. I need her. I want her. But my heart cries out for answers to this situation, he kept thinking. He knew the only thing he could do was confront her and talk to her so she could explain why she acted the way she did. He was just afraid that he might lose his temper, causing it to become a screaming match. But he had to try to understand why. He needed answers sooner rather than later.

He pushed the covers off of his body and sat at the edge of his bed, rubbing his face with both hands. His head hurt. A rush of hope filled him. He got out of bed and walked into the bathroom, immediately turning on the hot water in the shower. *Maybe the water will clear my mind*, he thought. He stood still under the hot water, his hands against the wall, his head bowed low to let the water soothe his body for several minutes.

Half an hour later Stephane felt revived. He dried off quickly and walked to his closet, where he chose a pair of Valentino blue jeans and a blue shirt. Using mousse, he slicked his hair back with mousse, then as he glanced at the mirror. He hadn't shaved, and there were dark circles under his eyes., *"I look like hell,"* he thought, and glanced away. He randomly grabbed a bottle of cologne off of the shelf next to the mirror and sprayed it on himself.. After slipping a pair of black Louis Vuitton loafers without socks, and he put a light jacket on. He grabbed his phone as he passed by the table and he shoved it into his pocket without looking at it, then headed toward the entryway of his condominium. In minutes, he was out of his building.

He walked slowly down one street after another, feeling the cool air of the morning on his face. The smells of the city and the sound of cars driving by didn't faze him. He kept on wandering until he noticed that he was only two blocks from Marcia's apartment. Stopping on the crossroads, he realized he was going to have to talk to her face to face. On the other side of the street, there was a vendor selling flowers from a cart. Stephane quickly walked over, then reached into his jacket pocket and took out his wallet.

"Bonjour, one dozen of red roses, please," he said.

He watched as the vendor wrapped the roses in clear paper and tied a pink bow around them.

"That will be ten euros, Monsieur," the man said after handing him the roses.

Stephane handed him the cash and thanked him, then turned on his heels and continued walking in the direction of Marcia's place as quickly as he could.

He slowed his pace when he saw her building. Taking a deep breath, he approached the front door and pushed the button for the intercom.

"Marcia, it's me. Please open up," he said.

He shifted his weight from one foot to another while waiting for Marcia to buzz him in, but there was no response. After he pushed the button again, still to no avail, he noticed that the front door of the courtyard was open. Taking the stairs two at a time, he went up to her apartment. Cold sweat dampened his back as he inched closer to her door.

Maybe she doesn't want to see me... Stop! Everything will fine. She loves you, he told himself.

He stood in the hallway, closed his eyes for a moment, inhaled deeply, and then took the last few steps toward her door. When he reached it, he realized that it was ajar.

"Marcia?" he said quietly as he lifted his hand and pushed the door open, immediately stepping inside. "Marcia, are you here? Marcia!"

As his eyes scanned the place, the roses dropped from his hand. A wine glass was shattered on the floor, a kitchen chair had been flipped, and dishes were scattered across the floor. He could barely breathe as he continued into the room.

"Marcia! Baby, answer me!" he screamed.

She was nowhere to be seen. His heart completely broke when he noticed the blood on the staircase. He ran up the stairs to check her bedroom, fear engulfing him. His whole body trembled at the thought of what he might find.

"Oh mon Dieu!" he screamed as he saw her lying on the floor, and he rushed over and knelt beside her. "Marcia," he whispered. "Wake up, baby, please."

He put two fingers against her neck and felt the pulse. A breath of relief escaped him, and he gently picked her up in his arms. Grabbing his phone from his pocket, he called 911, requesting an ambulance right away.

"Who would do such a thing? I will kill whoever did this. Please, God, just let her live," he said out loud, tenderly stroking the bloody hair from her face.

"Marcia, I'm here. I'm not leaving. Please wake up," he sobbed as he cradled her in his arms.

He looked down at her and saw that she had a cut above her lip and that one of her eyes was almost swollen shut. Her shirt was torn at the shoulder, and he could see bruises on her arms. Suddenly she moaned, then slightly opened her eyes and looked up at him. He saw a tear roll down her cheek.

"It's okay, baby. I'm here, and an ambulance is on its way. Just stay with me. Everything is going to be okay. I won't leave you. I'm so sorry," he said softly.

She closed her eyes, and he glanced toward the window briefly, hearing sirens coming their way. *Hurry! Please hurry*, he thought.

Finally, he heard a man yell, "EMT!"

"Over here...upstairs...hurry," Stephane shouted in the man's direction.

He could hear footsteps coming up the stairs, and then two men appeared in the doorway. They were dressed in white and blue uniforms and had multiple medical bags on their shoulders. One of the paramedics advanced toward Stephane and kneeled near him.

"Monsieur, excuse me. Please set her down flat on the floor and move away so I can examine her. What happened here?" the older man asked.

Stephane tenderly placed Marcia on the floor, then moved away so the paramedic could care for her.

"I don't know what happened. I found her like this when I got here about ten minutes ago," Stephane said as he watched the paramedic listen to her heart.

The man looked into her eyes with a light, then tended to her bruises. Lifting her head slightly, he placed a thick collar on her neck. Stephane sat at the edge of the bed, completely in shock. He couldn't think straight.

"Who would do such a thing to her? I should have been with her last night. It would never have happened," he mumbled to himself over and over as guilt set in.

"We need to transport her to the hospital right away. Get the stretcher," the man said to the other paramedic.

Stephane watched as the younger man disappeared down the stairs.

"Will she be okay? Is she going..." Stephane trailed off, a lump catching in his throat, his eyes filled with water.

"She'll be okay. She has a concussion and a few scars and bruises—nothing that won't heal. The good news is that her jaw doesn't seem to be broken. The doctors can give you more information. She'll live," he answered.

Stephane looked at him, then wiped his tears away. His mouth was dry, and he had a painful headache. Stephane just sat there in shock. All he could look at was her bruised face.

A few minutes later the other paramedic arrived with a flat board to transport her on. They gently lifted her up and placed her on the board, then strapped her in. Both men picked up the board and began to walk away with her.

"What hospital are you taking her to? Can I ride with her? I don't want her to be alone," Stephane said as he stood up and took a step toward them.

"I'm so sorry, Monsieur. Ambulance policy says you can't ride with us. We are taking her to the emergency department of Hotel Dieu Hospital. It's on Place du Parvis de Notre Dame. You can meet us there. I'm sure the hospital will need more information, and there is a police officer downstairs who wants to talk to you before you leave," the paramedic said.

"Please take care of her. I'll be there shortly," Stephane answered.

He noticed that there were two gendarmes in the living room as he followed the paramedics to the courtyard, and then one of them accompanied him from the apartment to the ambulance.

"Excuse me, Monsieur," he heard the policeman say, but he ignored him.

Stephane wasn't interested in talking to them at that moment. He kept following the medics, watching until Marcia was secured in the vehicle and sent off to the hospital. His teeth clenched together while he watched the blue lights of the vehicle disappear around the corner. People from the neighboring apartments and more gendarmes dressed in blue uniforms were gathered around the building, but Stephane paid no attention to them until he felt someone touch his arm.

"Excuse me, Monsieur. My name is Inspector Roland Poirier, and I'm with The Police Nationale of Paris. I would like a moment of your time to ask you a few questions," a man's voice said.

Stephane turned to face a clean-cut man in his forties. He flashed his badge at him, but Stephane didn't say a word. He just stared at him for a moment, uninterested. He didn't have the patience or time for the gendarme.

"I need to get to the hospital. I don't know anything. Can it wait?" Stephane answered sternly, then took a step to the side, trying to get to a point where he could either flag down a cab or get to his car.

"Monsieur, we can talk here, or we can go to the Seventh Arrondissement Police station. It is up to you. I have questions, and I need answers," the inspector said in a persuasive tone.

The gendarme pointed to a less populated area and place to the side of the entrance. He lifted his eyebrows at Stephane, then took his notepad out of his jacket pocket, motioning to the side of the building. Stephane slowly took a few steps toward where the gendarme was telling him to go.

"Now, first of all, what is your name, Monsieur? And how do you know the victim, Mademoiselle Philips?" the inspector asked, holding his pen and tablet in his hand while waiting for an answer.

Stephane swallowed hard before he answered him. He checked the time on his watch, annoyed that he couldn't leave and follow Marcia to the hospital.

"My name is Stephane LaRoche, and Marcia Philips is my girlfriend," Stephane answered quickly. He watched as the man wrote down the information on his pad. Stephane looked over the inspector's shoulder for a taxi.

"Do you have identification, Monsieur?" the gendarme asked.

Stephane dug his wallet out of his pocket and passed him his driver's license without a word. Inspector Poirier wrote down the information on his notepad and passed the ID back to him.

"I understand you are the one who found her and called the ambulance. Is that correct?" he asked.

Stephane nodded at him, shifting his weight from one foot to another, annoyed at him for the delay.

"So, tell me what happened here this morning? Did you have a disagreement and..." Poirier asked him.

Stephane felt heat rise to his face at the implication that he might have hurt Marcia.

"I would never hurt her in any way. I don't know what the hell happened here this morning. All I know is that Marcia is hurt, and that's how I found her. I think you should be out there looking for the bastard who did this to her. Stop wasting my time and let me get to the hospital so I can be by her side. If you have more questions, you can direct them to my attorney. His name is Monsieur Francois Letourneau, and he's on rue Saint Germain. He is listed in the phonebook. Bonjour," Stephane told him in an unpleasant tone.

He had just turned around and started walking away when he heard the inspector say, "I shall be in touch soon, Monsieur LaRoche. Don't venture too far."

Chapter 13

Marcia watched in terror, her eyes wide open, as Mason walked in and locked the door behind him. Her whole body shook from fright, as she had no idea what might happen if she couldn't control the situation. She swallowed nervously and took a step backward. Mason stood at the door, blocking the exit. He looked around her place, then grinned and began walking toward her.

"Well, you are early. I wasn't expecting you for at least an hour. Why don't you make yourself comfortable while I get you a glass of wine, and then I'll go upstairs and freshen up," Marcia said, watching as he shook his head and pouted his lips. *Stay calm. Smile. Don't make him mad,"* she kept telling herself.

"You look delicious just the way you are, darling. Where is your little friend?" Mason asked, taking a step forward again.

His eyes were all over her body. He was only about five feet away from her, and she could feel dampness crawling down her back.

"Oh, she just stepped out. She should return soon. How about a glass of wine to relax while we wait for her?" Marcia asked. She was lying, but she would do anything to keep him occupied until she could call Stephane again and tell him to come rescue her. Not waiting for his response, she turned around and walked to the small icebox in the kitchen. Opening the door, she grabbed the half-empty bottle of wine from the shelf. She reached in the cupboard and got out two wine glasses, then placed them on the countertop. The next thing she knew, his filthy hands were on the bare skin of her waist, his hands creeping up her blouse. A sense of loathing came over her, but she just giggled nervously and gently pushed his hand away.

"Let me pour you a glass of wine. Then I'll freshen up and be right with you," Marcia said as pleasantly as she could. She grabbed the glasses and the wine bottle and started walking toward the living room area.

"I don't want any fucking wine. That's not what I'm here for. If I wanted a drink, I'd go to the fucking bar," Mason replied as he snatched the bottle and glasses from her.

He threw them on the table and reached for her once again, but Marcia took a step back, avoiding him like the plague. She unconsciously brought her hands up, anticipating what might happen. He frowned, and she noticed his anger rise even more. His face was turning pink, and he frowned angrily at her, his fists turning into balls.

"What's the matter with you? You make me come here, and now you don't want me? Come here, you bitch!" Mason said, irritated.

Marcia backed away, taking a step to her right. *Oh my God! This was a huge mistake. How stupid of me to think I could ever outsmart or overpower this monster. I'm in big trouble*, she thought. She kept her eyes glued to him, and suddenly he lunged forward to grab her. She quickly moved to the left, causing him to miss her, and he bumped into a wooden chair, knocking it over. He scowled at her furiously.

"You whore!" he shouted.

"Mason, stop! Please! You need to calm down. Just let me freshen up and put something nice on, and I'll be right back," Marcia said as she kept backing toward the bedroom stairs.

"You fucking bitch! You think you can play games with me, don't you?" Mason screamed at her.

He rushed forward, and before she could say anything else or put her hands up in defense, she felt a blow hit her left eye, causing her whole body to crumble. Her head went backwards, her legs gave way, and she stumbled into the wall. She heard the breaking of glass as a picture on the wall fell to the floor. Closing her eyes momentarily from the pain, she tried to get her bearings.

"That will teach you not to fuck with me," he said.

She looked up and she saw the stairway to her bedroom right in front of her. Gathered all of her strength, she swiftly started to climb the stairs, but when she was halfway up, she felt a hand grip her blouse from behind. She knew that if she didn't react and do something, Mason would hit her again, so she turned around and kicked him hard while supporting herself with the bannister. Her foot hit his shoulder, and she heard him fall backwards down the stairs. She watched in horror from the top of the stairway as he winced in pain, then proceeded to get up.

"You little whore! I'm going to rearrange that pretty face of yours," he said as he stared up at her with his beady eyes.

Marcia screamed and quickly ran to her bedroom, not looking back. She slammed the door and reached over to lock it, but he came plowing through the door, overpowering her strength. Shrieking loudly, she ran toward the bathroom, but she tripped on the ottoman, lost her balance, and fell on the edge of the bed.

In a second he was on top of her, pinning her down with his knees. His filthy hands tore her blouse. She lifted her hands up in defense, then hit him as hard as she could, but it didn't seem to hurt him. He raised his fist and punched her one more time in the face. Pain radiated all throughout her head and body. She scratched and clawed at him, but he pinned her hands down. It seemed that the more she resisted, the more the blows came. He hit her in her ribs, and she realized that she didn't have anything left in her.

Suddenly she heard Stephane's voice on the intercom. She tried to scream, but nothing seemed to come out. All went black, and she lost consciousness.

Pain...so much pain everywhere. Oh my God, Marcia thought. She tried to open her eyes to see where she was, but her gaze was blurry. Pain shot through her side as she tried to sit up. The discomfort was too much, so she rested her head on the pillow again, not moving.

"Marcia! Marcia, can you hear me? It's Stephane. You're safe. You're at the hospital," she heard Stephane's voice say in her head, and she felt a soft touch on her right hand.

She tried to speak, but her throat was parched. "Water," she managed to whisper.

"Here, baby, just take small sips," he said.

She opened her eyes a bit as she felt the straw on her lip. The water soothed her dry mouth.

"Where am I? What..." Marcia asked in a weak tone, unable to finish her sentence as she remembered Mason. Just the thought of that man made her nauseous. She moaned in pain as she tried to move her head. She couldn't see Stephane, but felt him touch her arm lightly.

"You're in the hospital," he repeated quietly. "You're going to be all right. I'm here, baby. No one is going to hurt you. I'm right beside you. Just rest. I'm not going anywhere."

She could hear his voice breaking, and a feeling of relief swept over her as it finally sunk in that he was there, that he had come to save her. A soft knock at the door pulled her from her thoughts.

"Come in," Stephane answered.

A middle-aged man came in and stood beside her bed, a chart in his hands.

"Bonsoir, my name is doctor Bourgeois. I'll be taking care of you while you are here. I need to discuss a few things with Mademoiselle Philips. Would you mind stepping outside for a moment, Monsieur, so I can examine her?" the doctor asked.

"No problem. I'll be right outside the door if you need me," Stephane said to Marcia, squeezing her hand gently.

Marcia slightly opened her eyes and watched Stephane as he stood up. He nodded at the doctor, then stepped outside, closing the door behind him.

"How are you feeling, Mademoiselle Philips?" the doctor asked her in a thick French accent.

She squinted. Just the sound of his voice made her head throb, but she managed to say, "My head hurts."

"Well, you are a very lucky woman. The x-rays that were taken when you arrived here show that no bones were broken from the blows you received. You do have a concussion and several contusions on your right eye and lower lip, but there's nothing that won't heal in time. We also did a series of blood tests and an ultrasound, and everything looks fine. The baby is all right."

Her heart began to race, and she felt like she was going to faint.

"What? What baby? I'm not pregnant! You must have the wrong person," Marcia said in disbelief. *No! He made a mistake. He has the wrong person! That's not me! A baby?* she thought. She kept staring at him, waiting for him to tell her it was an error. He rechecked her paperwork.

"Mademoiselle, your blood test came back positive, and based on the ultrasound that was preformed upon your arrival, you are approximately six weeks pregnant," the doctor said, reconfirming his findings.

Her mouth opened, but no words came out. She was shocked. Hoping he was wrong, she tried to remember her last menstrual cycle, but her mind wasn't working. Her head pounded, and all she could do was nod at him.

"I will be keeping you overnight for observation, and if nothing arises, you will be free to go home tomorrow. I'll advise the nurse to only give you a low dose of pain medicine because of the baby. Try to sleep. You need to rest for the baby. I will check on you in the morning," the doctor said, then turned to leave.

When he was about to reach for the door handle, Marcia asked, "Doctor, who else knows about the baby?"

He turned to face her, answered, "Just you, Mademoiselle," and gave her a smile.

"Doctor, could you not mention my pregnancy to anyone?" she asked.

"Absolutely, it is your decision. I will not say a word," he answered, then proceeded to exit the room.

Marcia closed her eyes. She was flabbergasted. It was all too much to process at that moment. She heard footsteps enter the room again and knew it was Stephane. She didn't want to look at him, afraid that she might burst out crying at any moment.

"Is everything okay?" he asked as he pushed a chair closer to the bed.

"Everything is fine. Why?" she answered quietly.

"You seem a little pale. Why don't you sleep? I'll be right here by your side when you wake up," Stephane said, rubbing her arm.

All she could do was turn her face away from him and give him a slight nod.

* * *

Stephane wiped a tear from his face with the back of his hand. He sat on the wood chair next to her bed, holding her fragile hand while she slept. One of her eyelids was so puffy that she barely could open it. Her lower lip was bruised, and she had a lump on her forehead. She looked completely helpless, but he knew she would be okay. He vowed to never leave her alone again. "What had happened to her? Who would want to hurt her? If he ever found out who did this to her was going to pay dearly," he thought as he pursed his lips as anger then guilt of not being there to help her swept over him. He laid his head on the side of the bed and closed his eyes.

Hours passed, but he did not leave her side while she slept. Every time Marcia would stir in her bed, he would look up at her. Later he heard a gentle knock on the door, and someone slightly opened it. He lifted his head up and saw the gendarme he had spoken to earlier. The inspector motioned for him to step outside the room. Stephane didn't want to leave her side, but he knew it would be better to talk in the corridor so they didn't wake her up. He carefully let go of her hand and got up from his chair, walking to the door. When he stepped out, Inspector Poirier was a few feet down the hall, leaning against the wall. As Stephane approached him, he stood up straighter.

"I'm so sorry to disturb you, Monsieur LaRoche, but the doctor told me I could talk to her. If I'm going to catch who did this to her, I need to ask her a few questions about what happened. Has she mentioned anything to you?" Inspected Poirier asked.

"No, she hasn't said anything. Do you have to question her now? Can't you wait a bit? She just fell asleep," Stephane said as he took a deep, annoyed breath. He kept his eyes on the inspector, hoping he would agree. Marcia didn't need an interrogation now.

"I really have no choice. I'll be as gentle as I can, but the longer I wait, the easier it will be for the suspect to elude us. It's better to do it now. She might remember something if it's still fresh in her mind," Poirier told him, then took a step to the side to pass him.

Stephane did the same and blocked his path.

"Fine, but I'm not leaving her side," Stephane said, frustrated.

The inspector nodded, and Stephane turned around and led the way to Marcia's room. They entered quietly, and Stephane approached the right side of her bed. His stomach clenched. It was hard for him to keep his emotions in check when he saw her looking so feeble. He took her hand in his and rubbed the top of it with his thumb, never taking his eyes off of her.

"Marcia, sweetie, could you wake up? There a Gendarme who wants to talk to you," he said, watching as she stirred a bit, her eyes fluttering open.

"This is Inspector Poirier from the Police Nationale," Stephane said, motioning toward the man standing at the end of the bed.

"Miss Philips, I understand you are tired, but could you tell me what happened at your apartment? Can you describe the person who harmed you?" he asked, waiting to write down her answers in his notebook.

Stephane noticed her eyes become glassy, and she shook her head.

"I don't know who it was," she whispered as a tear fell.

"There was no sign of a break in. Did you let him in? Maybe it was a delivery man or a neighbor?" Poirier asked, continuing to question her.

Marcia just stared at him for a moment, then shook her head. "I must have...forgotten to lock my door." Marcia said then turned her head away from him.

"Can you describe what he looked like or what he was wearing?"

"I don't know. I don't remember him. He was a big white man." Marcia said without looking at the gendarme.

"What color was his hair? Any tattoos or scars you can remember?"

The inspector persisted. Marcia shrugged and shook her head.

"That's enough for today. She needs to rest. You can talk to her when she feels better. Now, please leave," Stephane said, intervening. He glared at the inspector as he raised his hand and wiped a tear from her cheek. It broke his heart to see her cry.

"Very well, but I will return. Keep in touch. Let me know if you recall anything at all," the inspector said, placing one of his card on her side table. He put his notepad and pen back into his jacket pocket and walked out.

"I'm so sorry. I don't remember," Marcia said quietly.

"Don't worry about it. It will be alright. Close your eyes and rest. I will be right here when you wake up. I love you," Stephane said, a lump rising in his throat.

That son of bitch who did this is going to pay dearly, he thought as he watched her close her eyes and turn her face away from him.

Chapter 14

Marcia's head was spinning. With all of the pain medicine they had given her, she could barely focus. She could sense that Stephane was standing beside her, and he touched her arm gently, then said her name. She opened her eyes and saw that there was a man standing at the foot of her bed, and when she noticed the badge handing from the chain around his neck, she figured out what was going on. The inspector asked her about what took place, but she couldn't tell him about Mason. *I can't tell him in front of Stephane. And what proof do I have anyway? Mason would deny ever being near my place. Stephane would never believe what occurred*, she thought. So she lied to the inspector. Feeling the need to rest and get her strength back, she closed her eyes after the gendarme departed and fell asleep.

When Marcia woke up the next morning, her whole being was aching and sore. She sat up and saw that there was a pitcher and a glass of water on the table near her bed. As she reached over and grabbed it, her ribs throbbed. She swallowed several mouthfuls of water.

She looked around the room and saw that Stephane was slumped over in a chair, his hair and clothes disheveled. He was sleeping. He had stayed with her like he had promised her earlier. Suddenly she heard a knock on her door, and her doctor came in before she could answer. He smiled at her, closing the door behind him. Stephane had woken up at the sound of the door closing, so he sat up straight in his chair, running his hand through his hair. When he glanced her way, he gave her a smile, but she could tell he was tired by the dark circles under his eyes.

"Bonjour, Mademoiselle Philips, I see you are feeling better this morning," the doctor said.

Marcia nodded as the doctor approached her bed, her chart in his hand. He placed it on the side of her bed, then took his stethoscope out of his pocket. He placed the end of it on her chest and listened to her heart. "Very good," he commented.

"Now I want you to follow the light with only your eyes," he instructed her, pulling a pen light out of his pocket. Leaning toward her, he made circular motions with the pen, then right to left movements, and Marcia obeyed and followed them as best as she could. "Well, there doesn't seem to be any permanent damage to your eyes. The swelling will go down in a day or so. It's more of a discomfort than anything else. Your vision might be blurry for a day or so. You also received a bad blow to the head, so you might have some headaches, but I do believe it will be okay. You just need to rest. I will prescribe something for the pain. I would like to reexamine you in a week, just to be on the safe side, or you can contact your own doctor."

"That's great news! When do you think she can come home?" Stephane asked, sitting at the edge of his chair.

The doctor turned and smiled at him. "She is free to go as soon as I finish the discharge papers. It will probably be a couple of hours or so. I would like you to eat something before you leave. Take care. Nice to meet you both."

"Thank you," Marcia whispered, but she didn't think he heard her, as he disappeared behind through door without another word.

Stephane came over near her bed and kissed her softly on the forehead.

I can't go home. Mason knows where I live, so he might come back, she thought. *What am I going to do? I can't defend myself if he comes back. Where am I going to go? A hotel?*" Marcia looked up at Stephane.

"I'm so happy that you are going to be all right. You don't need to worry about anything. Don't cry! I'm not going to leave you alone. Whoever did this to you will never hurt you again. I swear," Stephane said softly, then reached over and wrapped his arms around her, hugged her tightly. She couldn't speak, so she just nodded at him. "First, you need to regain your strength, so you have to eat. I won't let you return to your apartment just yet. I want you to stay with me, at least until you feel better and get back on your feet. Plus, that way, I can keep an eye on you and spoil you."

Again, she couldn't speak, so she just nodded, a tear rolling down her cheek. She turned her head away from him so he wouldn't notice it. *He solved my problem for the time being, but I know that it is only a temporary fix. His sister is engaged to that bastard. There is no way to avoid Mason. Stephane is trying very hard to reassure me that everything will work out, but he has no idea what Mason is capable of*, she thought. She felt him pull the cover over her shoulder.

"Get some rest. I'll wake you up when we can go home," he said, sitting back down in the chair by her bed.

Darkness had settled over Paris by the time Marcia received her discharge papers. She sat in the passenger seat of Stephane's Bentley and stared out the window, a prescription for pain killers in her hand. She was wearing blue scrubs that the nurse had given her, as the inspector had taken all of her clothes for evidence. As they drove down the street, she watched the people walking on the sidewalks and the buildings passing by. Stephane had not mentioned anything about the dinner incident. She now felt embarrassed at how she had behaved, but she hadn't had much choice.

"Stephane, about the other night at dinner—" Marcia said quietly, but before she could finish apologizing, he cut her off.

"It's forgotten. Don't say another word. It's in the past," Stephane said. She touched his hand, and he smiled her way. "I'm just glad you are coming home with me so I can take care of you. The first thing I'm going to do is run you a warm bath. It will make you feel so much better. And while you are soaking, I'm going to whip us up something to eat."

"That sounds perfect."

She turned toward him and gave him a small smile. He parked the vehicle close to the entrance, then jumped out to come help her. After opening her door, he extended his hand to her, and she placed her hand in his and got out. Within minutes she was in his home, sitting down on the sofa in the living room. She inhaled deeply and looked up at him.

"Just relax! I'm going to run you a bath. I'll only be a second," he said, leaning over and kissing her on the cheek, then disappearing into the bedroom.

She was relieved to be out of the hospital, safe with Stephane. At least she wasn't alone, so she didn't have to worry about Mason.

Her focus right now was to get her strength back and reserve her attention for herself.

"All set!" she heard Stephane say as he approached her. "Let's get these garments off. I got one of my shirts out for you to wear for the moment. We can get you something else to wear when you feel better." Stephane said to her.

"Thank you. I really appreciate it."

Marcia stood up and slowly walked to the bathroom, with Stephane in tow. Every step she took made her body ache. She noticed that he had lit candles by the tub. The bath had bubbles, and the room smelled like roses. She smiled at his thoughtfulness. He helped her take her top off, then dropped it on the floor. Slowly she bent down and pulled her pants off, and when she looked up, she noticed that Stephane was watching her every move. Although she didn't feel like it, she still gave him a full view of her breasts and unhurriedly placed her feet in the water, then finally slid down under the bubbles. The water felt warm, and it was soothing her aches. She glanced up at him and saw the corners of his mouth lift in a sensual smile. Although he looked exhausted from spending the night caring for her, he was still beautiful. One side of his shirt was sticking out of his wrinkled trousers. The shadows under his eyes and his messy hair told her how much he must love her to have stayed by her side.

She knew he wanted to touch her, so she said, "Why don't you come over and wash my back?"

She leaned forward slightly and heard him groan quietly, which caused her to giggle. He immediately took a step forward, rolling up the sleeves of his shirt, and knelt next to the tub. She picked up the soap and a washcloth, handing them to him. His touch was gentle and slow, putting just enough pressure on her back, almost like a delicate massage. Not a word was spoken for what seemed like an eternity. She could feel his breath on her neck, his caresses going up and down her back.

"Why don't you unwind while I fix you something to eat. You must be starving. You haven't eaten much today. How does that sound?" he asked as he pulled away from her, sitting back on his heels.

"As much as I want you to continue, I do believe you are right. I could use a bite to eat. Thank you again," she said, then slid herself down farther into the water.

"My pleasure. I am here to serve and obey," he responded, laughed lightly.

He came forward and kissed her on the cheek, then stood up and disappeared into the other room.

* * *

Stephane had just finished scrambling two eggs with vegetables in a saucepan when he saw Marcia come out of his master bedroom. She had a white towel wrapped around her wet hair and was dressed in his oversized shirt. Instantly he felt an erection grow at the sight of her. Even with a bruised face, she was the perfect woman. He didn't move; only his eyes followed her as she sat down at the counter.

"I feel so much better. And I'm hungry," she said, smiling at him, causing his heart to melt.

"I'm glad. I don't cook for just anyone. My cooking isn't that great."

He grabbed a plate and turned around, placing the eggs on it. He set the masterpiece in front of her, and she giggled as she looked at the plate, covering her mouth with her hand.

Stephane felt embarrassed as he looked at the eggs, but she picked up her fork and ate everything.

That night they cuddled close to each other in his bed. He gently swathed her with his arms, not letting her go all night. Her body stayed close to his, and he could smell the scent of her hair, which made him happy. With his arms wrapped around her waist, he closed his eyes and went to sleep, content that she was safe.

The next day Stephane heard his phone ring. He slowly pulled his arm away from Marcia and reached over to his night table to grab his phone. Glanced at the clock radio, he saw that it was six o'clock in the morning. The sun was barely up. *Who's calling me this early?* he thought as he slowly sat up on the edge of the bed.

"Allo," Stephane whispered while rubbing his face with his left hand, trying to wake up.

"Allo, Stephane, it's Reginal. Your father asked me to call you. There's been a slight accident at the house."

Stephane had known Reginal since childhood, as he was one of the foremen at the winery as well as a friend of the family. Through the phone, he could hear people shouting in the background.

"What happened? Is everyone okay? Did anyone get hurt?" Stephane quickly asked, then waited impatiently, his foot tapping on the floor.

"Your sister had an accident. She fell down the stairs at the house, but she will be fine. She just has a few blacks and blues. Your parents wanted me to call you. She will be okay."

Relief washed over Stephane.

"Mon Dieu! Are you sure she is all right? Let me talk to her!"

"The doctor was called, and he is tending to her. She said she tripped on her dress. Your mother and father are with her."

"Okay, tell Father that I'll be there as soon as I can."

Stephane turned around and glanced at Marcia, noticing that she was awake. She yawned, and he smiled at her, motioning for her to give him a minute. She nodded at him without saying a word.

"Very well, I shall tell him," Reginal said, and then Stephane heard a click on the phone.

He sighed, relieved that Etienne wasn't badly hurt, then put his phone down. Slipping back under the covers, he wrapped his arm around Marcia's shoulder and pulled her close to him. Her head leaned on his chest, and she lifted her head from his chest to look up at him.

"What was that all about? Is everything okay?" she asked, her eyebrows furrowed.

"Yes, there was an accident at the house. Etienne fell down the stairs. She's okay...only a few bruises. Someday, I swear, she's going to really get hurt. She is so clumsy. Half the time she doesn't look where she walks. But she's fine," Stephane said, annoyed at being woken up because his sister was accident-prone. He lay back in bed as he snuggled closer to Marcia, wanting to forget the phone call, at least until the afternoon.

"What? What are you talking about? What happened?" Marcia asked as she pulled away from him to sit up in bed. She rested her back against the headboard. He pushed himself up and sat next to her. Her eyes staring at him while she waited for answers.

"Reginal said she tripped on her dress. Her shoe must have caught the hem, so she stumbled down the stairs. We can go home later today and see her. She's all right. Now, since we are both awake..." he answered, carefully pulling her on top of him.

He could feel her delicate breasts rubbing against his torso, and an erection immediately began growing against her. He kissed her lips very gently, not wanting to hurt her. She pulled away slightly, nodded, and then smiled down at him. His whole body came alive as she moaned, and he tenderly rolled her on her back and began kissing and licking her neck, making his way downward.

Chapter 15

Later in the day Marcia felt rejuvenated and stronger. Her bruises were healing, and her black and blues had turned yellow, which meant she could cover them up with makeup. She sat next to Stephane in his car, on her way to face her worst enemy: Mason. This time she would not fail. She didn't have a plan yet, but she would figure out a way to either destroy him or expose him. They had been driving for about two hours in the countryside. Her head rested against the headrest, her eyes were closed, and her left hand was resting on Stephane's thigh while he drove back to Epernay. The sound of jazz music resonated in the car. She pretended to sleep so Stephane wouldn't bother her, but her mind was in a whirlwind about the baby and Mason.

I wonder if Etienne fell down the stairs or if Mason might have had something to do with her fall, she thought. *I have to be extremely careful about this evil man, especially now that I know I'm pregnant. I won't jeopardize the baby by getting hurt again. But what if Mason decides to hit me again? No, I'll find a way out. But what if Mason pushed Etienne? Shouldn't I help her before he harms her? Should I tell Stephane about Mason, and what about my pregnancy? If I speak up, my past will come into play and I will lose the love of my life. I can't bear to think about that. What to do? Maybe I could talk to Etienne and try to warn her about Mason without exposing myself. But how? And when? Who can I trust?"* she thought.

"Marcia," she heard Stephane say, and he put his hand over hers.

She opened her eyes and glanced at him, then turned her head toward the window. They were passing a small village with rows of houses that were probably built in the 1800s. There were bungalows made of yellow stone, and they had red clay roofs, wood fences, and lots of flowers in the yards. She also noticed vegetable gardens on the side of the houses, along with several sheep grazing in the back fields. The hills in the background were full green fields with grapes growing in rows. There were emerald vineyards everywhere. *How beautiful and picturesque! I can understand why Stephane lives here,* she thought.

A tiny sign by the side of the road indicated the town: Epernay. She felt a rush of nervousness come over her at the thought of seeing Mason again, and her heartbeat began to pound faster. There were too many questions and not enough answers. She closed her eyes momentarily to calm her nerves. Her eyes filled with water, but she blinked them away. She felt a hand rubbing her thigh again, and she turned her head.

"Hey, sweetheart, what are you thinking about? You have been so quiet. We are almost home," Stephane said as he continued to drive through the narrow streets.

"Oh, not much. I was just enjoying the ride," she answered as cheerfully as she could, smiling at him.

She reached down and grabbed her pocketbook, then placed it on her knees, taking out her makeup bag and mirror. She examined her face and cringed, then proceeded to camouflage her bruises with more concealer before putting her sunglasses on.

"Babes, you look beautiful! After a couple of days of my mother's cooking and some time with me, you are going to forget everything and be as good as new. I will always be by your side. You are safe, and no one is going to harm you at my parent's house."

Stephane massaged her leg, and she snickered softly. *Little do you know... You are such a good man*, she thought.

She straightened herself up in the seat and said, "Maybe that's just what I need: a good homemade meal." She decided she would find the answers she needed as she went along and just enjoy her time with him, for now.

Fifteen minutes later they were driving up the driveway to his parent's home. Stephane parked the vehicle in the front yard and jumped out, and his mother came running out of the house. Her arms opened wide as she approached Marcia and gave her a hug.

"I'm so glad you are okay. Stephane told me what happened. That was so awful! I'm so sorry. If there's anything you need, please let us know. Now come inside and have something to eat with us," his mother said.

"Thank you for having me," Marcia replied as she stood by the car. She felt a warm feeling of belonging with his family.

Stephane's mother turned and gave her son a hug and kissed him on the cheeks. She took Marcia's hand and led her inside, heading toward the kitchen. Stephane grabbed the bags from the trunk and followed them in, dropping them at the entrance, where Reginal picked them up.

"Come sit down. I prepared a delicious lamb stew," his mother said, motioning for Marcia to have a seat at the table.

Marcia obeyed her without a word, but not before she glanced around to see if Mason was nearby. Stephane came and sat next to her, and she was glad he was with her. He picked up a roll from the basket on the table and took a bite.

"How's Etienne?" Stephane asked his mother as he ate.

"She is much better. She will be happy you are home."

They watched as his mother took two bowls from the cupboard and scooped large portions of stew into them, and then she placed them in front of Stephane and Maria.

"Eat," she said as she pulled a chair out and sat down next to her son. "That girl...I swear, she is so inattentive! She is fine, just a few bruises, but she could have badly hurt herself. She fell down the whole flight of stairs." She gestured again for them to eat. "Mangez before it gets cold."

Marcia was famished, so she picked up her spoon right away and tasted the stew. It was delicious. They talked a little about the vineyard while they devoured their food.

"I hope you are going to stay for a couple of days. I miss having my son around the house. It will be nice to have the whole family here for dinner. I was so sorry to hear about your attack. How are you doing? Do the police have any leads?" Stephane's mother asked as she picked up the empty dishes in front of them.

Marcia watched her silently, wondering if Mason was at the house. She couldn't see past the kitchen area. Mason travelled a lot, so she hoped he was away. It had only been three days since he had put his filthy hands on her. She raised her hand and gently touched her cheek. It was still sensitive—a reminder of what had occurred.

"No leads yet, but I'm feeling much better now, thank you. Stephane has been taking good care of me."

Stephane stood up and walked over to his mother. He kissed her on the cheeks and said, "We would love to stay a few days. It will give Marcia time to recuperate and spend time with Etienne. Thanks for lunch. It was mouthwatering, as usual. I'll take Marcia upstairs to my bedroom so she can rest, and then I'll go check in on Papa."

"Very well. Marcia, if you need anything, please don't hesitate to ask."

"Thank you so much," Marcia answered.

Stephane came over and took her hand, winking at her. "Come on. I'll take you up to my room."

She gently slapped him on the arm, then followed him up the stairs and to his bedroom. He opened the door and let her in. A mahogany, four-post, king-sized bed stood in the middle of the room, adorned with a gold coverlet and lots of colorful pillows. Two large windows faced the green fields of the vineyard, and she noticed a marbled bathroom to her right. Stephane closed the door behind him, and she walked to the windows to admire the view.

"What a beautiful view!" she said as she gazed out the window. Suddenly she felt a warm body pressing against her back and arms wrapping around her waist. A wet kiss on the back of her neck made her smile. She tilted her head to the right, closed her eyes, and relished the moment. Hearing him quietly moan, she giggled and pivoted so she was facing him.

"Now I'm going to have dessert," he whispered as his tongue slid down her neck.

Marcia giggled, then tenderly pushed him away. "It's not that I don't enjoy this, but I think you should let me unpack while you go see your father first. I'm sure he knows you are here and is anxious to see you. We will have lots of time to fool around later." Marcia said to him.

He pulled away slightly and grinned at her. "Okay, I suppose you are right. I do need to talk to my father. I won't be long, and I will be back in half an hour for my dessert." Stephane joked.

Marcia nodded, giving him a grin, and his hands glided to her butt, squeezing it gently. He kissed her one more time on the lips, then moved away from her.

"I'll be waiting!" she said, watching as he took a few steps toward the door then stopped.

"Etienne's room is down the hall, on the left, if you want to say hello. I'm sure she'll be delighted to have company. I'll be back."

Stephane disappeared behind the door, and Marcia stood still, examining the room for a moment. She turned toward the window and looked down into the courtyard, noticing the man she despised so much: Mason.

An ice cold chill ran down her back, and she rubbed her arms with her hands. She stared at him with hate as he walked up to a man and exchanged a few words. He turned and headed back inside the house, then unexpectedly looked up toward the window she was standing at and smirked at her. Marcia immediately took a step back and hid behind the silk drapes that graced the room as memories of the attack came back to her.

She swallowed hard. *I will destroy you, you bastard, for what you did to me and Tiffany, even if it's the last thing I do. I will find a way. I'm not afraid of you*, she thought. She walked to the bathroom and looked at herself in the mirror. After a moment of thinking, she decided to go talk to Etienne. She wanted to try and get information about her fall because she believed Mason had something to do with it. Along with that, she also wanted to see how Etienne was doing.

As she walked down the hallway, it was like she was walking on a cloud. Not a sound could be heard from the old wooden floors as she stepped on them. She could see Etienne's bedroom door down the hall, and it was ajar. Voices could be heard as she approached. She took one more step before becoming paralyzed from the sound of his voice. It was Mason. He was in the room with Etienne. She put her back against the wall and listened to the conversation. She could hear Etienne whimpering softly, but she didn't dare glance inside the room.

"I didn't mean what I said last night. It was a silly argument. Let's just forget about it. It was an accident. I never meant to push you down the stairs. I was angry, and it will never happen again. You understand, and you know how much I love you. I want us to get married. I would never intentionally hurt you. I love you! Can you ever forgive me and get past this stupid quarrel we were having? I'm so sorry," Mason pleaded.

Marcia raised her hand to her mouth and sucked in a breath. She was right; he had pushed Etienne down the stairs. Glancing down the hallway, she made sure she was alone before continuing to listen to them.

"I love you so much, and I want to spend my life with you. I'm sorry too. I should never have doubted you. It was all my fault, and as you said, it was an accident," Etienne said.

Marcia couldn't believe how manipulative Mason was. Etienne was so naïve, unable to see past his charms.

"I'll let you rest for now. Maybe we can go for a ride through the countryside and grab some lunch this afternoon, just me and you," Mason said.

Marcia heard someone coming up the stairs, so she scurried back as quietly as she could, moving away from Etienne's bedroom door and headed back to Stephane's bedroom. She opened the door quickly and closed it behind her, putting her back against the door and waiting, listening for any sound. She held her breath. Her heart began pounding in her chest when she heard footsteps outside her door. The sound of a knock made her jump back. She stood there, frozen, just staring at the door.

"Mademoiselle Marcia, it's Reginald. Can I come in? I have your bags."

A rush of relief ran through her, and she reached for the doorknob and opened the door for him. "Yes, please come in." After he placed her and Stephane's luggage in the room, she thanked him, giving him a nervous smile.

"You are most welcome. Monsieur Stephane asked me to inform you that he is in the library having a glass of wine with his father. You can join them if you'd like."

"Oh, merci! Well, could you tell Stephane I will join him in a few minutes. I just want to see how Etienne is doing, and then I'll come down in about fifteen minutes."

"Very good." He walked out, leaving the door open.

She took a step forward and checked the hallway, looking for any sign of Mason. After Reginald disappeared down the stairway, she looked toward Etienne's room. *I have to talk to her now, before she has time to think about what Mason said. I have to try and expose him for what he is: a women beater,* she thought. She ventured out toward Etienne's door and knocked gently.

"Yes, come in," Etienne said.

Marcia opened the door, putting a smile on her face. Etienne was propped up with pillows on her bed, dressed completely in sweats. An ice pack was on her ankle, and she had a magazine on her lap. Her bedroom was decorated in white, with the exception of a multicolored pastel fabric that accented the room. Marcia advanced toward her and sat in the white chair beside her bed.

"Bonjour, I just wanted to see how you were feeling and if you needed anything. Stephane told me you had a fall. I was so sorry to hear that," Marcia said. She noticed that Etienne's eyes were puffy, most likely from crying.

"That's so nice of you to be concerned, and check up on me, but I'm fine. I only bruised my ankle. I'll be up and about in a day or so. Ice will cure anything," Etienne said, trying to be unconcerned about the situation as she pointed to her ankle. She gave Marcia a weak smile.

"So, tell me what happened. You fell down the stairs?"

Etienne looked around the room for an instant, as if she was thinking about her response.

"Yes, clumsy me! I tripped on the hem of my skirt and fell. Nothing to be alarmed about. It was an accident." Etienne said calmly.

"Were you alone when you fell?"

Marcia's question seemed to agitate her. She rubbed her hands together and looked at Marcia.

"Yes, unfortunately, I was. Mason heard me scream when I fell and came to help me."

Marcia moved to the edge of her seat and reached over to cup Etienne's hands in hers.

"Etienne, you know I'm very fond of you and that I only want the best for you. Earlier today, when I was coming to see you, I heard a conversation between you and Mason. I know you didn't fall down the stairs. You were pushed."

Etienne pulled her hands away. "You were listening to our conversation?!" she exclaimed angrily. Then her facial expression changed, and she pursed her lips and narrowed her eyes on Marcia. "Whatever you heard was between me and my fiancée. It has nothing to do with you. Mason loves me. It was an accident, and it would be better for you to keep your mouth shut. I will deny anything you say. Now get out of my bedroom." Etienne said then turned her face away from her.

"Etienne, let me explain. Please let me help you. I've seen this behavior in men before, and he will hurt you again. He's trying to control you, and he's not the right man for you," Marcia said, but she could see that Etienne wasn't going to listen.

"How dare you! This is none of your business, and you know nothing about Mason. It's your word against mine. Get out of my room, now!" she screamed.

Marcia stood up from her chair and shook her head at Etienne. "Okay, I'm leaving, but I'm here if you need me."

* * *

Stephane sat in one of the leather chairs across from his father as they both sipped on glasses of wine. He couldn't stop looking at the two oak doors that led into the library. *I wonder where Marcia is.? What is keeping her?"* he thought. Reginald had mentioned that she was going to visit Etienne, but she should be arriving soon, since that was over half an hour ago. He heard his father chuckle, so he turned his attention back to him.

"You like this girl, don't you? You haven't stopped talking about her since you arrived, and now you keep watching those doors and waiting for her to come through them. It reminds me of when I was dating your mother. I couldn't wait to be with her, and I never wanted to leave her side," Stephane's father said, laughing at his son.

"You know, between me and you, I love Marcia. I want to ask her to marry me. But don't tell Maman, or she will tell everyone. One wedding at a time."

"Yes, I understand. Speaking of weddings, is everything all right between Etienne and Mason?"

"Why do ask that? Is something wrong? I don't know Mason that well. I'm so busy with work, and now Marcia, and I haven't had time to discuss anything with Etienne."

Stephane got up to pour himself another glass of wine, then walked back and sat next to his father again.

"It's just that Etienne seems edgy lately. I heard them arguing the other day. It must be the wedding jitters. I don't think anything significant, but..." His father trailed off, smiling as he looked toward the doors, and Stephane turned his head and saw Marcia walking into the library.

"Hey, I was just wondering where you were. Would you like a glass of wine?" Stephane asked, rising to greet her. He kissed her on the cheek, then took her hand and led her back to where his father was sitting.

"That sounds great! How are you, Monsieur LaRoche?" Marcia asked politely as she took the glass of wine that Stephane had poured for her. She sat down in one of the chairs close to Stephane's father.

"I'm well. Thank you for asking. How are you feeling? We were so worried when Stephane told us about the break-in at your apartment."

"I'm healing nicely. You have an excellent collection of novels. I love books," Marcia said, changing the subject.

"Yes, I like to read when I find time. You are most welcome to pick out any of the books you feel like reading." After gulping down the last drop of his wine, he placed his empty glass on the side table and stood up. "Well, I'll leave you two love birds alone. I need to get back to work. Marcia, it's always a pleasure to see you, and welcome to our home."

Marcia thanked him, and he nodded at her before walking out, leaving the two of them alone. Stephane noticed that she was being quiet and that her attention seemed to be elsewhere. She was staring out the window as if she had something on her mind. He placed his drink down on the table, then reached over and rested his hand on her knee. She turned and smiled at him.

"Is anything wrong? You seem distant." He watched her take a sip from her drink, avoiding his gaze. "Marcia, what's the matter? I know you by now. I know something is bothering you. Maybe I can help." he asked her softly.

She glanced into his eyes. He waited, but not a word was spoken from her lips. She turned her head away from him again, and his heart sank because she was holding something back. He knew she was upset.

"Marcia, did you see Etienne? Did she say something to upset you? She can be a little spoiled some days and say things without thinking," Stephane said. He gently rubbed her knee and waited, and she turned and faced him.

"I need to tell you something..." Marcia said, then paused for a moment as she took another drink of her wine.

"Babes, I'm listening. You have all my attention." He wondered what it could be that would make her so nervous. She pulled herself to the edge of her chair and leaned toward him as if she didn't want to be overheard.

"This morning, on my way to go see Etienne, I overheard a conversation between her and Mason. I was standing by the door of her bedroom and..." Marcia said, then hesitated. She bit her lower lip and cast her eyes away from him for a moment, glancing at the open doors of the library. Stephane took both her hands in his and held them.

"It's okay. Tell me what you overheard. Were they fighting again?" Stephane asked while never taking his eyes off of her. He gave her a minute to gather her thoughts, as she seemed to be debating if she should tell him or not.

"I don't want to get anyone in trouble, but I heard Mason apologize for pushing Etienne down the stairs. He said he was angry about something, that they were quarreling and that he didn't mean to push her down the stairs. He said it was an accident. Mason said he loved her and still wanted to marry her. He told her it wouldn't happen again." Marcia whispered to him.

"What? Are you sure that is what you heard?" Stephane said quickly. He felt Marcia's hands tremble a bit in his, but he held them firmly as his anger began to build inside him. He could feel heat rising down his back. He clenched his teeth tightly, unable to believe Mason would do such a thing, especially to his little sister. "How could he? I should have been here to protect her."

"That's not all."

Stephane inhaled deeply and held it so that he didn't explode before knowing what else she had overheard. He waited quietly.

"So, after I overheard this, I didn't know what to do, so I thought I could help. I confronted Etienne with this information. She told me to mind my own business, that she would deny anything I would say to anyone and that it wasn't true. Then she told me to get out of her room. I'm sorry. I didn't know what else to do. I thought you should know," Marcia said, bowing her head.

"You did the right thing. I'll have a chat with Etienne. Let's see what she says. I'll ask her about her accident, and then I'll know if she is lying. I know her too well." Stephane said, he let go of her hands and rose. *I'll kill the son of a bitch if what Marcia says is true. How could he do such a thing?* he thought.

"Stephane, please don't mention it was me who told you. I don't want her to blame me, or cause friction between you two."

He looked down at her. She was his angel, and he would never implicate her.

"Don't worry, I'll take care of this. Wait for me here. Why don't you finish your wine. I won't be long," Stephane told her as calmly as he could, trying not to let on that his stomach was in a ball of fire. He leaned down and kissed her on the mouth, turned around, and quickly exited the room. He marched swiftly down the hall and went to the stairway, taking the stairs two at a time up to Etienne's room. When he got to the top of the stairs, he stopped for a moment. He held the bannister tightly trying, to compose himself, trying to figure out how to approach this situation. Going in there and accusing Mason of pushing her down the stairs would be fruitless. First of all, she would know Marcia told him and would contradict everything, even though he already knew the truth. He closed his eyes momentarily and inhaled, looking down the hallway at Etienne's room.

He spun around, then ran down the stairs, headed to the foyer downstairs. As he scanned the area, he was looking for one person only. He saw Reginal through the large glass windows of the backyard and headed out the door.

"Reginal," he shouted in his direction as he approached him. Reginal was on his way to the warehouse with a toolbox in one hand. He turned and waved at Stephane when he heard his name.

"Bonjour, Monsieur LaRoche." Stephane walked up to him.

"Bonjour, Reginald, I'm looking for Mason. Have you seen him?" While his eyes swept the backyard of the estate.

"Oui, oui, I just saw him. He was under the pergola making phone calls a moment ago. Did you want me to tell him you are looking for him?"

"No, thank you, Reginald. I'll find him," Stephane answered, then followed the path to the garden. He spotted Mason sitting in a lounge chair, talking to someone on the phone, a glass of wine and a cheese plate in his lap. Stephane headed in his direction, and Mason waved him over. *Whatever you do, keep your cool if you want to catch him in his lies*, Stephane thought as he sat down next to him on the other chair. Mason quickly finished his conversation on the phone and placed the phone next to him.

"Bonjour, I heard you had arrived. Have a glass of wine with me, maybe some cheese." Mason said nonchalantly. He poured Stephane a glass, then offered it to him. Stephane took it from him and thanked him.

"It's a beautiful afternoon for a little relaxation," Mason said, lifting his glass in a toast to him.

"Yes, isn't it so unfortunate Etienne couldn't join us. I was told she fell down the stairs. What happened?" Stephane asked, then took a mouthful of wine, trying to ease the anger that was building inside.

"That woman...I love her dearly, but somedays, I swear, she is so uncoordinated. She tripped on the bottom of her skirt. Thank goodness she didn't hurt herself any more than she did." Mason said then chuckled. He picked up a piece of cheese and popped it in his mouth.

"I hear you were with her when she fell."

Mason's demeanor changed slightly. He stopped chewing his cheese for an instant, then swallowed.

"Yes, I tried desperately to catch her, but I was unsuccessful. An unfortunate accident."

Mason drank the last drops of his wine, then poured himself another glass. Stephane watched him closely while trying to find the right words to question him.

"What were you and Etienne arguing about before she fell?" Stephane asked Mason, never taking his eyes off of him. Mason scowled at him.

"Who told you that? I would—" Mason blurted out then sat upright in his chair. Stephane interrupted him before he could finish his sentence. Stephane edge closer to Mason on his chair, Mason fidgeted nervously.

"So, you were arguing. Are you sure you did your best to catch her, or were you angry and you pushed her down the stairs?" Stephane asked in a harsh tone as his right hand balled into a fist.

"What are you implying? I would never. Who has been spreading lies?" Mason asked, looking irritated by Stephane's words.

"They are not lies. Someone overheard your conversation this morning, you bastard. You pushed her down the stairs, and you hurt my sister, you piece of shit."

Stephane lunged forward and grabbed Mason by the collar of his shirt with both hands. His face was inches from Mason. Mason raised his hands and tried to free himself from Stephane's grip, but it was too firm.

"That's not true. Ask Etienne. She will tell you differently," Mason said as he tried to defend himself, beads of sweat dripping from his forehead. Stephane knew at that moment that what Marcia had overheard was the truth. Mason was lying.

"Yes, she would protect you and say anything because she loves you, but this is what is going to happen. You will break off your engagement with my sister—the sooner, the better—and disappear; otherwise I will tell her I know. I will inform my parents too. I don't give a fuck what you tell her, but this wedding is off, or you will regret the day you ever met me," Stephane said between clenched teeth as he stared him straight in the eyes. "Either I will have you arrested, or she will mourn you at your funeral. Do you understand?" Stephane thrusted him back in his chair. Stephane stood above him, glaring down at him then he took a few steps back.

"Was that someone who told you these lies your slut girlfriend?" Mason spit out at Stephane. Rage engulfed Stephane at the foul name he had called Marcia. He whipped around with balled fists.

"What did you say?"

"I said, was it your bitch telling you lies?" Mason snickered.

Stephane leaned forward, and his right fist hooked Mason's eye so fast that he didn't have time to shield the blow. The punch was so fierce that it cut Mason's eyebrow, causing blood to run down his cheek. Stephane's body trembled from rage at his words.

"You fucking asshole. How dare you hit me. You will pay for this," Mason yelled as he touched his eyebrow.

"Leave this house immediately," Stephane managed to tell him before he punched him again. He turned on his heels and walked away from him, going back toward the house.

When he was a few yards away, Stephane heard Mason scream in his direction, "Why don't you ask your whore what her profession was while in college? You might be surprised how she paid her tuition."

Stephane stopped walking for a second, took a long breath, and exhaled, his fists tight. He shook his head, then continued on his way toward the warehouse. He needed to calm down.

Chapter 16

Suddenly Marcia felt sick to her stomach. She sat back in her chair so she could rest her head back, then closed her eyes, hoping the nausea would pass. *It must be the wine and all the excitement of the morning*, she thought. It was getting worse. She opened her eyes and scanned the library for a bathroom, but there were none to be found. Rising quickly, she hurried out of the room, down the hall, and into the nearest bathroom. She swung the door open and ran inside, where she began to throw up in the toilet bowl. When she finished, she grabbed the towel from the counter and ran cold water on it. As she began to wash her face and neck, the coolness of the wet towel helped her feel better.

Realizing that she needed to either return to her room to lie down or go outside to get some fresh air, she decided that the afternoon sunshine might cure her. She slowly walked toward the outdoor garden, scanning the grounds for Stephane—or worse, Mason. But neither were around. She saw two lounge chairs under a large oak tree overlooking the vineyard. *Perfect! I'll wait there for Stephane to get back from talking to Etienne*, she thought. After she sat down in the chair, she closed her eyes and tried to relax. The warm breeze caressed her face as she stretched out, and she fell asleep.

She was startled when she woke up and she heard someone screaming. Opening her eyes, she tried to focus. Etienne was standing at the foot of her chair. Her eyes were red, and tears were rolling down her cheeks. She looked extremely mad.

"You fucking bitch! You couldn't keep quiet your mouth shut, and you told Stephane everything, and now my life is ruined because of you. Mason broke off our engagement and is going back to America. I'll make you pay for this one day. You must be happy," Etienne said angrily with her hands on her hips. Marcia sat up, shocked and speechless. She looked up at her, trying to find the right words.

"What are you talking about? Oh...I'm so sorry, Etienne. I never meant for this to happen, but Mason...he's not—" Marcia said, but Etienne cut her off.

"Shut up, you whore! Don't even mention his name. Mason told me all about you, how you worked for an escort service during college and slept with every man who paid you. You messed around with the wrong person. I'm going to tell Stephane all about you. He won't want you when I'm done with what I'm going to tell him, bitch!" Etienne spit out at her.

Marcia's head throbbed with pain. She couldn't breathe. Her secret was out. Mason had spilled everything about her past. She stood up and extended her hand toward Etienne, but Etienne slapped her hand away.

"Don't touch me, you wench. You don't deserve my brother. He will leave you when he finds out what you are. I'm going to tell him everything!" Etienne screamed at her. Eyes glaring at her.

"Etienne, listen, you might not believe me, but that life is in the past. I've changed. Mason is an evil man. He's dangerous. I know him. He pushed you down the stairs. He's the one who beat me up, and he would've hurt you again. I know you don't understand it, but it's the truth. Please, I beg you, don't tell Stephane. I never meant to cause you pain," Marcia pleaded, her heart pounding in her chest at the thought of losing Stephane.

"I don't believe you, you hoe! It was an accident. He didn't push me. You will pay for this, I swear. Your life with Stephane is over. I want you to suffer like I'm suffering," Etienne hollered. She turned around and began running toward the house, wailing uncontrollably.

"Etienne, please don't tell Stephane. Let me explain," Marcia yelled. She took a few steps toward her, but Etienne didn't listen; she just kept rushing back toward the house. Suddenly a feeling of nausea rushed through Marcia again, and her legs became weak. Her head was spinning, and she was lightheaded. She tried to steady herself by grabbing the back of the chair, but it was to no avail. Her legs gave way, and her vision blurry, everything went black.

"Marcia, wake up! Marcia!"

Marcia heard a familiar voice. Someone was gently shaking her. She slowly opened her eyes and looked up at Stephane. He had a worried look on his face. After picking her up in his arms, he placed her back on the lounge chair she had been lying on before. She was in a cold sweat, and her skin was clammy.

"What? What happened?" Marcia asked in a daze. She looked around, trying to remember what was going on, and then she remembered. Etienne was going to tell Stephane about her.

"Are you all right? I found you on the ground next to the chaise. You must have fainted," Stephane said as his fingers pushed the hair off of her face.

Marcia sat up and scanned the area quickly. Etienne was nowhere in sight. She looked up at Stephane, and tears pooled in her eyes. She didn't know what he knew. *Had Etienne told him yet? Should she confess to him about herself and try to explain?*

"I'm okay," Marcia said slowly. She wrapped her arms around his neck and embraced him hard. She wanted to feel close to him one more time before everything fell apart and he left her. Tears rolled down her face. "I love you so much," she whispered.

"I love you too, babes. Don't worry. I'm right here. I think we should get you checked out. You are so pale. There's a doctor in town. His name is Dr. Antoine Lucien, and he's an old friend of the family. I'm taking you there right now. It's not normal that you fainted. No arguments!"

The baby. I hope the baby is all right. What am I going to do? I need to tell him I'm pregnant with his child, she thought.

He helped her up and put his arm around her torso as they walked toward the car. Marcia surveyed the area again. She didn't see Mason or Etienne, so she exhaled a sigh of relief. He opened the door of the car, and she sat down, still feeling a weak. She watched as he ran around to the other side of the car and opened the driver's door. Marcia's mouth opened when she saw Etienne coming out the front door of the house. *Oh my God!* She was paralyzed with fear.

"Stephane, wait, I need to talk to you. Where are you going? It's important. Stop! Stephane," Etienne shouted in his direction as she came down the steps of the veranda, waving at Stephane frantically as she tried to keep him from driving away.

"I'll be right back. I need to go to town," Stephane yelled back, hopping in the car. He started the engine and began backing out of the driveway.

Please keep going. Don't stop. Don't listen to her, Marcia thought as she gripped the door handle tightly and avoided his gaze. She couldn't think. She prayed he wouldn't stop to talk to her. *Please not now!*

"No, stop! I have to talk to you. It's about your Marcia," Etienne screamed desperately, but Stephane didn't stop; he put the car in drive, and it rolled down the driveway.

A sense of calm swept over Marcia when they were at the end of the driveway. She exhaled deeply, tears flowing down her cheeks, knowing she only had this small amount of time left with her only love before he cast her aside. He would never understand what she did to survive when she was younger, and he would never forgive her. She looked at the house one last time in the rear mirror as they disappeared down the path, knowing she would never set foot in that home again.

"Marcia, please don't cry. It's going to be just fine. Dr. Antoine is a great physician. He's a childhood friend of mine. He will find out why you fainted. It's probably just stress from the break in," Stephane said to her. He reached over and rubbed her thigh softly.

They drove the short distance to town in silence. Marcia had no words. She was in shock at the events that had happened with Etienne. They arrived at a small, country, stone house near town. The house had a red roof and a yellow door, with green pastures behind it. There were two pots of pink flowers near the doorway. A wooden sign hung by steel brackets on a post by the front door read:

"Dr. Antoine Lucien, general practitioner." Stephane parked the car in the narrow driveway, and then his phone rang. Marcia jumped at the sound of the ringing.

"Please don't answer "she whispered. He picked it up and looked at the caller ID. Marcia bit her upper lip nervously, knowing it was Etienne who was calling him.

"It's only Etienne. I'll call her back later," Stephane said, pushing the voicemail button, and then he placed his phone back in the cup holder.

I have to tell him the truth before anyone else does. That's the only chance I have to make him understand, she thought.

He opened his door and came around to help her out. They walked the short distance to the door and entered a tiny reception area. An older woman sat behind a desk, a partition dividing the two rooms. There were four wooded chairs as well as a table with magazines, a picture on one of the walls, and a coat rack in the corner. Stephane and Marcia walked up to her, and the woman smiled and greeted them.

"Bonjour, Stephane. How are you? What can I do to help you?" the woman asked him as she glanced at Marcia.

"Bonjour, Murielle, I'm well. Is Antoine in? This is my girlfriend Marcia. She fainted this morning, and I wanted him to examine her to make sure she's okay."

"Yes, as a matter of fact, he is. I'm sure he'll be happy to see you. He's just finished with a patient. I'll tell him you are here. Please have a seat. I'll be right back," Murielle said. She pointed toward the chairs in the reception area, then disappeared toward the back of the office. By now Marcia had stopped crying and just stood by Stephane, waiting. He stroked her back gently.

"Everything will be okay. Don't worry," Stephane reassured her, but all Marcia could think of was if the baby was okay. They turned around and went to sit down on the chairs in the reception area. Marcia's leg bounced up and down nervously while she waited in silence. Murielle reappeared at the counter a minute later.

"This way, please," Murielle said. Marcia and Stephane stood up together to go see the doctor, and a tall, dark-haired man in his late thirties appeared in the hallway. He came toward them with arms open wide and gave Stephane a hug.

"Stephane, my friend, so nice to see you. You are a busy man. I haven't seen you in months. How are you?" Doctor Antoine asked, then glanced over at Marcia.

"I'm just fine, thanks, and you?" Stephane asked, then turned and looked at Marcia. "This is my girlfriend Marcia. She fainted this morning, and I was wondering if you had a minute to check her out and make sure she's okay." Stephane said then put his arm around her waist.

"Well, nice to meet you, Marcia. I'd be glad to examine her, so if you will follow me..."

Stephane took a step forward. Marcia touched his arm and said, "Would you mind if I saw him alone? I'll be fine. I'd rather do that." Marcia said to Stephane who raised his eyebrows at her in surprise.

"Are you sure?" Stephane asked her, concerned.

"Yes, I'm a big girl. It shouldn't take long anyway," Marcia said, then kissed his cheek and stepped away from him before he could object again.

"Okay, I'll be right here if you need me." Stephane said then returned to sit on the chair. He snatched a magazine from the table and started leaf through it.

Marcia followed the physician into an examining room, and Doctor Antoine closed the door behind him.

"Have a seat on the table and tell me what the problem is," he said calmly. The room was simple, only having an examination table, a chair, and a desk. Marcia did as she was told and hopped up on the table, then placed her hands on her lap.

"Thank you. I'm not sure what happened this morning, but I think I fainted. I blanked out. Stephane found me. And I was concerned. As you might have noticed, I have a few bruises on my face. Someone broke into my apartment a couple of days ago. I received a concussion and..." Marcia trailed off, bowing her head as she thought about the baby. Doctor Antoine came toward the table.

"I'm sorry to hear that. Let me take your vitals so we can find out why this happened."

Marcia watched in silence as he took his stethoscope from around his neck, then checked her heart and lungs. He then took her blood pressure and pulse and examined her eye and bruises. When he was done, he walked to his desk and made a few notes on a piece of paper.

"Do you have any pain anywhere, or are you on any medications?" he asked her. Marcia shook her head.

"Your blood pressure is a little high, but nothing to worry about. Let me ask you, are you stressed about some matter? Or do you have anxiety problems?"

"I have been strained. Could that make me faint?" Marcia asked, although she already knew the answer.

"Yes, it could, but it's probably from the concussion. You need to relax for a week or so, and I would recommend a healthy lifestyle. If it happens again, I could prescribe some medication for the stress...

a mild anxiety medication. But other than that, you seem to be in good health."

"I'm also about six weeks pregnant. Could it have hurt the baby?" Marcia blurted out without thinking. Dr. Antoine stopped writing, smiled, and looked up at her.

"Congratulations! I suspect Stephane is the father. He must be elated with joy. He has always wanted children," Doctor Antoine said, and Marcia nodded. She nervously bit her lower lip, looking away from his gaze.

"It's not good for the baby for you to be so stressed out, but it won't affect the baby unless it keeps happening over and over. So I suggest you learn to unwind. Maybe you could take vitamins, and make sure to keep your obstetrician informed."

Marcia nodded and thanked him.

"I'll walk you out so I can reassure Stephane that both you and the baby are okay," he said, then opened the door for her. Her heartbeat spiked a beat when he mentioned telling Stephane.

"No, no, you can't tell Stephane about my pregnancy. He doesn't know yet. I would like to tell him myself, surprise him this weekend," Marcia whispered while walking back to the waiting room.

"No problem. I won't say a word. I'm sure he will be delighted," he answered. Marcia felt relieved that the baby was fine and that Antoine would not tell Stephane. Stephane stood up when he saw Marcia walk into the room.

"How is she?" he asked immediately as he glanced back and forth between his friend and Marcia. He wrapped his arm around her torso.

"She's fine. No worries at all. Just try to make her rest and relax more, that's all. It's probably from her concussion from the break in," the doctor answered him.

Marcia kept quiet while the two men chitchatted about old times and getting together soon. *I have to tell him the truth about myself and the baby, especially now that I know that the baby is okay. My God! What am I going to do? If I don't explain the situation to Stephane, Etienne will be able to tell him all the vicious lies Mason told her. She's furious at me for breaking up her engagement. She will want her revenge. What story will she conjure? I won't have a chance with Stephane. But I love him too much. I have to try to keep him,* she thought. Her mind was in turmoil.

"Thank you so much, Antoine, for taking care of my girl and reassuring me she's okay. Let's meet up for a drink and catch up soon. Send the bill to the vineyard," Stephane said as he extended his hand to shake Antoine's.

"Don't worry about it! That sounds great. I'll give you a call next week," Dr. Antoine said, then turned around and headed back to his office.

Stephane and Marcia walked back to his car. Marcia hadn't said a word since she had left Dr. Antoine's office. Stephane glanced at her and reached over to stroke her hair, but she didn't turn to face him. She knew he was trying to figure out what was bothering her, but there was no way he could even imagine what she had to tell him.

"I'm so happy you're fine. I think we should take it easy the next couple of days and relax, like Antoine said. We can return to the house and—" Stephane said, but before he could finish his sentence, the phone rang again. He reached down toward the cup holder to pick up the phone, but Marcia covered his hand firmly.

"Please don't answer. I need to talk to you about something that's very important first," Marcia pleaded, looking him directly in the eye.

"Okay, what's the matter? What do you want to talk about? Let's return to the house first, then—" He removed his hand from the phone and let it ring. He didn't answer.

"No, not the house. Could we go somewhere quiet? I want to talk to you privately, with no interruptions. It's important."

"Sure, are you all right?"

"Yes, I'm okay," she answered. She turned her face toward the window without another word.

* * *

A few minutes later he parked the car on Avenue de Champagne, near a park by the town hall. It was a tranquil place. There were benches and large trees for shade, and not too many people were present.

"How about we go for a walk in the park?" Stephane suggested, and Marcia nodded. The silence from Marcia was killing him inside. *Worried, he hurried out. "I hope she's not going to tell me she is leaving me. I can't live without her*, he thought. He reached out for her hand while they walked, but she pulled away and put her hands in her pockets. He glanced down at her, but she was staring straight ahead. They strolled down one of the paths until Marcia sat down on one of the benches. Stephane sat next to her and waited for her to speak. All that could be heard were the birds chirping and a dog barked in the distance, He turned his body toward her.

"All right, please tell me what is so important that we can't return home. I can't stand your silence anymore. It's driving me crazy," he said.

Her head was bowed, and her hands were on her lap. He reached over and took her hands in his, but she didn't look up at him. Tears rolled down her cheeks, and she covered her face with her hands and wept.

"Babes, I love you with all of my heart. There is nothing you can tell me that we can't resolve together. Please tell me what's the matter," Stephane begged her, then waited patiently for her to speak.

Chapter 17

"Stephane, I love you more than life. First, I want you to promise me you won't interrupt me or say a word until I'm done talking," Marcia said with tears in her eyes. She closed her eyes and took in a deep breath.

"Okay, I'm listening, babes. There isn't anything you could say or do that would make me not love you," Stephane said softly.

"There's a lot you don't know about me. I want you to keep an open mind. I need to tell you about myself and why I came to Paris," Marcia said, then paused. She glanced up at Stephane, who nodded and gave her a weak smile. She bowed her head again, as she couldn't look at him while she talked because she wouldn't be able to continue she felt so ashamed. *"It's better that he hears the truth from you rather than from his sister. God knows what lies she might tell him,* she thought.

"As you know, when I was in college, my parents passed away and I was having difficulty making ends meet financially, even while working two jobs. That's when I met Tiffany during my junior year. I was going to drop out of college–that's how bad it was. I needed to find a way to make money, so as you know, I went to work at her place of employment."

She paused for a second, and he squeezed her hands lightly, letting her know he was listening. She could barely breathe, so she opened her mouth and sucked in some fresh air to give her courage.

"I had no other choice. I needed to survive, so she introduced me to the life of escort services."

Stephane pulled his hands away from hers. He crossed his arms against his chest and sat back against the bench. Marcia didn't move; she just stared straight ahead, rubbing her hands together while she tried to find the inner strength to go on. *He's not pleased, but he's still here, so you need to carry on, please forgive me*, she told herself.

"I worked for two years, saved money, and then quit after I graduated. That's how I met Mason."

Stephane slid away from her on the bench, his eyes widening with horror, but he stayed seated, not speaking.

She continued, "He was a client of Tiffany's, and his fetish was to hurt girls. When I found out that he was going to marry your sister, I couldn't let that happen, so I tried to stop him. Mason was the one who beat me and Tiffany up. I came to Paris to start a new life, and then met you." She turned toward him, but his face was without expression. "Stephane, I never meant to cause you any pain. I love you too much. I'm so sorry. I should have told you sooner, but I was afraid you wouldn't understand and that you would leave me."

Marcia sobbed. She raised her hands to hide her face again and began to weep. She could feel that Stephane was still next to her, but he wasn't saying anything.

"Please say something. I can't bare the silence anymore. I have told you everything," Marcia said and looked up at him. All she could see was hurt in his face. His eyes watered, and he shook his head, standing up. She reached for his hand, but as soon as she touched it, he pulled away quickly and shrugged her off.

"Please, I'm so sorry about everything, I love you so much. Don't...leave me," she sobbed in-between words.

Still, he didn't utter a word. She watched as he stood up and marched away from her. He turned the corner and disappeared, going back to his car. He never glanced back at her. *He didn't love me enough to forgive me*, she thought.

Hours passed, and she sat on the bench in a stunned state, unable to think or move. She had no more tears. Finally, darkness fell, and there were less people around. It was unbearable. She was exhausted, and her whole body hurt. Her heart was forever broken. She had lost the love of her life. *He couldn't even look at me. He was probably disgusted by what I have done to survive. I will never hold him again or make love to him*, she thought. She needed to get back to Paris. She couldn't stay in this town. There were too many bad memories. Using her last ounce of energy, she pulled herself up from her seat and staggered out of the park, heading in the direction of the bus terminal.

* * *

Stephane drove for hours through the streets of Epernay, his vision blurred by tears, trying to comprehend what Marcia had just confessed to him. *How could she deceive me that way? All the lies? An escort service? Mason? What a fool I was to think she loved me She's been using me all along. Why didn't I seen the signs? Did she really love me, or was I just another one of her clients?* He pulled into the parking lot of a local pub, needing a drink to take some of the pain away, possibly to make him forget what had been told to him. He got out of his car and blindly walked into the bar. He passed a row of leather booths that were filled with patrons enjoying drinks. French music played in the background. He sat down on one of the stools at the main bar and immediately flagged down the bartender at the other end of the counter. Stephane could hear people talking and laughing around him, but he didn't care; he just wanted to drown his pain and forget Marcia forever.

"Bonsoir, Stephane, what can I get you?" the bartender asked him as he wiped the bar area in front of Stephane with a cloth.

"Whiskey, straight. Make it a double, please," Stephane told him. He watched as the bartender turned around and faced the many alcohol bottles on the shelves behind him. He grabbed a bottle and poured a drink, placing it in front of Stephane, who gulped it down in one swallow. He grimaced. He could feel it burn as it went down his throat and into his stomach. He pushed the glass toward the bartender.

"Another one. As a matter of fact, leave me the bottle," Stephane said to him.

"Stephane, you know I can't do that. It's against policy," the bartender said calmly.

"Then keep filling my fucking glass," Stephane said angrily, then guzzled the second drink. After several more drinks within the span of an hour, Stephane was feeling the alcohol taking effect. His elbows were against the countertop, and he was slumped over his drink, staring at the empty bottles in the bar. He was drowning his feelings at the bottom of a bottle of whiskey, trying to feel nothing, trying to forget her, even if it was only for one night.

Stephane lifted his head when he heard a familiar voice behind him. His jaw tightened, and his hands formed into fists. Anger invaded his soul. Repulsed at what he had been told by Marcia, he pivoted on his seat. Standing a few feet away was Mason. He was talking to a woman as if his fiancée had never existed. He was flirting with her. Mason's back was turned away from Stephane. His laughter enraged him.

"Mason was the one who beat me up, and he pushed your sister down the stairs." Marcia's words echoed in his head.

Stephane stood up and walked toward him, then shouted, "You fucking asshole, I told you to leave this town."

Stephane pounced on Mason. He grabbed the back of his jacket and swung him around with all of his strength. Mason lost his balance and went flying into a table and chairs next to him. He fell to the floor, bleeding, as he had hit his head on the corner of the table. People moved to the side. Stephane laughed at him, then took a few steps forward, bent down over him, and picked him up. He held on to him with one hand, using the other hand to hit Mason on the side of the head. Mason lifted his hands in defense, but they were useless. The surprising blow had incapacitated him. Stephane punched him again, giving him a blow to his jaw and one to his temple. Mason's head swung sideways, and his eyes rolled backwards in his head. He looked like a rag doll being pushed around.

Stephane screamed at him, "You fucking bastard, you like to beat on women. Pick on someone your own size. Coward!"

Stephane went to hit again, but someone gripped his arm and pulled him away.

"Stop, Stephane, that's enough. What is the matter with you?" Doctor Antoine asked.

Stephane pulled his arm sideways, trying to free himself so he could get back to Mason, but another patron came forward to help drag Stephane away and stop him from harming Mason. Stephane glanced down at Mason, who was lying on the ground, his face bloodied and his shirt ripped. Stephane wiped his mouth with the back of his sleeve. "You deserve more than a beating, asshole. Go back to where you came from, women beater!" Stephane yelled at him.

A man helped Mason sit up on a chair. It seemed that Mason was trying to understand what had occurred while trying to get his bearings. People gathered around to see what was going on.

"You are nothing! Crawl back under your rock," Stephane spit at him in-between heavy breaths. Stephane watched as one of the servers helped Mason up and walked him out of the establishment.

"Calm down, my friend. That's enough. Let's sit down and talk," he heard Doctor Antoine tell him. Stephane brushed his shirt off and took the few steps back to his barstool. He sat down, looked at the bartender, then pointed at his drink.

"One more, and send me the bill for the damaged furniture," Stephane said to him. The local bartender didn't object; he just poured him another drink. Stephane felt someone pat him on the back. He glanced over his shoulder at the person who had taken a seat next to him. It was Doctor Antoine. Stephane took a mouthful of his drink and examined his knuckles, which were slightly swollen from the blows. He didn't care; he felt better.

"What was that brawl all about? It's usually not you who picks a fight. He must have pissed you off royally," Antoine said.

Stephane just ignored the question. He didn't feel like talking about it. Stephane just took another sip of his whiskey, and grunted irritated at his friend for breaking up the fight.

"Well, I didn't think we would be meeting so soon for a drink, especially under these circumstances," the doctor said, then motioned the bartender over. "I'll have a beer. I hope that's your last drink tonight. Finish it, and I'll drive you home. I don't think you should be driving." Antoine told him then took a mouthful from his beer.

"I'm not going anywhere. Leave me alone," Stephane said. He finished his whiskey and motioned to the bartender for another. By now Stephane could barely focus. He turned to his friend, but his vision was playing tricks on him. He was seeing his double of his friend. He tried to refocus, then started laughing uncontrollably. He embraced his friend while trying not to fall off his stool.

"Come on. I'll drive you home. It's on the way to my house anyway," Antoine said. He took one last drink from his beer and placed it on the counter. Stephane fumbled to pay the tab, finally throwing two hundred euros on the bar. Antoine helped Stephane stand and walked him outside. Stephane wrapped his arm around Antoine's shoulder.

"Get in," Antoine ordered him when they arrived at his vehicle. Stephane didn't object; he quietly slumped in the passenger seat and watched as Antoine got in on the other side.

"Antoine, please, I don't want to go home. Let me sleep over at your house tonight," he managed to mumble.

"Okay, I'll take you to my place, but only for tonight," Antoine said, laughing. Stephane leaned his head against the window and closed his eyes. The next thing he knew, he was lying on Antoine's couch, and he fell into a drunken sleep.

The next morning Stephane stirred in his sleep. The rays of the sun from the window in the living room shined brightly in his face. His head hurt, and he opened his eyes slightly, then closed them again. He rolled on his side, trying to shield his face from the bright light. He almost fell off the couch.

"Good morning, buddy, rise and shine," Antoine said to him cheerfully. Stephane sat up on the edge of the sofa and glanced up at his friend. He placed his elbows on his knees, then rubbed his face.

"Here, take this," Antoine said. Stephane looked up at him. In one hand he held a cup of coffee, and in the other were two pills. Stephane reached over and took the coffee and the two pills from him. He popped the pills into his mouth, then took a sip of the hot beverage. He grimaced when the hot liquid went down.

"Thanks," Stephane said, and then he sat back and rested his head on the back of the couch. His head was pounding with pain. Antoine sat next to him with his own coffee.

"The painkiller will help that headache in a few minutes. That was a hell of a fight last night. I don't know what's going on, and it's none of my business, but don't you think with a baby on the way you should try to set a good example for your child and stay out of jail?" Antoine chuckled.

"What? What did you say? What are you talking about?" Stephane asked as he lifted his head to look at him, shocked and confused.

"Oh no...I thought..." Antoine became quiet, not finishing his sentence, and Stephane tried to comprehend what he had just heard.

"Antoine, what child? Are you telling me Marcia is pregnant?" Stephane said, he no longer felt the pain of his headache, he was wide awake, he needed to confirm what Antoine had said. He took a drink of his coffee while he waiting for an answer.

"I'm sorry, man. I thought you knew. She told me she was going to tell you, so I assumed she had told you last night and that you were upset about it. I thought that was why you were drinking."

Stephane's mouth dropped open to speak, but nothing came out. His hands began to shake, and he spilled some of his drink on the floor.

Marcia is pregnant with my child? Why didn't she tell me? I'm going to be a father, he thought. A dark cloud came over him as he remembered how she confessed everything to him and how he pulled away from her. If he had been more understanding, maybe she would have told him about the baby, but then he had left alone her in the park.

"That's all right, Antoine. You didn't know. Thanks for taking me in last night, but I have to go find Marcia," Stephane said to his childhood friend. He put his beverage down on the coffee table, stood up, and hugged Antoine, then headed toward the front door.

"Call me later," Antoine shouted as Stephane ran toward the exit.

He had to find Marcia. He closed the door behind him without a word.

* * *

Marcia had grabbed the last bus to Paris the previous night. She sat on her bed at her apartment. The tears had stopped. Her mind was still in shock at losing Stephane, but while on the bus ride home, she had made the decision that she would return to Boston. Marcia spent hours on the phone with Tiffany, crying and recounting the events of her day. Tiffany was compassionate. She was excited about the baby and was going to help her raise her child. She offered to take her in until she found a new place to live. Marcia realized she had to move on and make a home for this baby. *Stephane abandoned me. He didn't want me.* Her heart was broken, but she would get over the man in time. It would be hard to put her life back together, but she had to think about the baby now. That was her priority.

She touched her belly with her hand. "It's me and you, kid. We will be okay," she said out loud as sadness came upon her again and her eyes pooled up.

She stood up, wiped the tears away, and zipped her last suitcase up. She had spent most of the night gathering her belongings. She hadn't slept much, only a few hours in the early morning, when she had fallen asleep on her couch after purchasing her airline tickets. She had called her landlord in the early morning hours to discuss the last months of her apartment lease. Now she showered and put on black jeans and an oversized sweater. Her whole body ached when she picked up and wheeled her suitcases out the front door.

She came back inside and took one last look at her apartment. She walked from one room to another, making sure she hadn't forgotten anything. She grabbed her carry-on and dropped her keys on the counter for her landlord. Taking the last few steps out the door, she closed the door behind her, never looking back. She waited patiently outside until she saw the taxi she had called roll up in front of her apartment.

"Taxi, Mademoiselle," the young man asked as he came out of his van. Marcia nodded. She stood by him as he placed her bags in the truck. Her dream of living in France and finding love had shattered. Now that her man was gone forever, she needed to concentrate on herself and the baby. The taxi driver opened the back seat door, and she slid inside. The man sat in the driver's seat and looked in his rearview mirror at her.

"Where to, Mademoiselle?" he asked politely as he started the engine and waited for directions. She glanced at her tickets and passport in her hand.

"Charles de Gaulle airport, Air France terminal, s'il vous plait," Marcia told him in a quiet tone, and then she turned her face away from him. She held the handle of her carry-on tightly, trying to stop tears from falling down her cheeks, but it was to no avail. Her vision blurred with water again. She watched the many famous buildings of Paris pass her by one by one until the city disappeared behind her. *Another chapter of my life is finished, but I have a new life growing in me, so I will be strong and persevere*, she thought, then touched her belly with her hand.

Chapter 18

Stephane ran to his car as quickly as he could. It was only a few blocks away. He finally saw his vehicle by the side of the road, in front of the pub, where he had left it the previous night. He sprinted the last few yards. Breathing hard, he grabbed the handle of the door, but the door didn't open. The car was locked. He frantically searched his trousers and jacket pockets for his keys, but they were nowhere to be found. He pounded on the hood of the car. He didn't have his keys; he had lost them.

He leaned against the car, trying to think clearly. He needed to get to Marcia. He pushed his hair from his face, took a deep breath, and let it out. Think! His mind was blurred. He took out his phone from his pocket and dialed Reginal's number. He tapped his foot impatiently as he waited for him to answer. Reginal answered after the third ring,

"Allo, Reginal, it's Stephane. I lost the car keys to the Bentley. I'm in front of the Bar Parisien in town. Could you come pick me up right away? I need to return to the house immediately," Stephane asked.

"Oui, Monsieur, I'll be there as soon as I can. Is everything okay?"

"Yes, Reginal, please hurry! I'm waiting," Stephane said, then hung up. He paced up and down the length of the car while he waited. It was only ten minutes from the house to the pub, but for Stephane it seemed like hours while he waited for Reginal. He had so many questions that needed to be answered. *Why didn't she trust me enough to tell me the truth? I should not have been so harsh with her. I should have been more understanding, and I should have left the past in the past. I should have been more patient and talked to her. She probably would have told me about the baby*, he thought. His mind was full of regrets. He looked at his watch impatiently. Fifteen minutes had passed since he had telephoned Reginal. He leaned against the car again to wait. *He should be here by now. Where the hell is he?*

He had dialed Marcia's number again, but to his despair, she didn't answer. He had called her number several times since he had left Antoine's house. There was always no answer. He put his phone back in his pocket. His headache was getting worst, he rubbed his temples. He noticed a familiar red truck coming down the street. He stood up straight and waved at Reginal, who pulled to a stop beside him. Stephane stepped out into the street and hopped in quickly, telling him to drive home quickly.

Stephane jumped out of the truck the minute they came to a halt in the driveway of his parents' home and ran up the house. He took the steps two at a time up to his room. He took his shirt off and threw it on the floor. He put on a clean sweater on, ready to go find Marcia. He turned around to leave but noticed Etienne was standing in the doorway, blocking his exit. Her eyes were red and swollen, as if she had been crying. Her clothes rumpled, and her hair a mess. She looked like she hadn't slept, and she was holding a half-full bottle of wine in one hand.

"Stephane, where have you been? I've been calling you, and you never answered. I need to talk to you. It's about Marcia," Etienne said to him. Her speech was slurred.

"I don't have time to talk to you right now. I need to return to Paris. Excuse me," Stephane said to her as he motioned for her to get out of his way, but she didn't move.

"Did you know Marcia was once a prostitute? You are dating a slut! A gold digger! A liar! She is the one who ruined my life, and she will do the same to you. Stay away from her," Etienne said angrily, not budging from her spot.

Stephane pressed his teeth together as outrage ran through his bones at her words. He didn't want to debate the issue now.

"Get out of my way!" Stephane snapped at her. "I don't have time for you right now." Stephane said angrily.

Etienne stood her ground. He pushed her to the side to get by her. "You knew, didn't you? You let that bitch come into our lives and disgrace our family. She made me lose the love of my life. You should be ashamed to be called LaRoche."

Stephane stopped walking abruptly. He whipped around, livid, his eyes slanted. Heat rolled up his neck, and he took a deep breath, trying not to lose control of his emotions.

"Disgraced? Ashamed? You bring home a man who beats women for pleasure, a criminal who you want to marry, and then you lie to protect him. Don't talk to me about honor. At least she put her life back together, so be very careful what you say, little sister, before you judge." Stephane lashed out her way then turned around to continue down the hallway, leaving his sister speechless and alone.

The next two hours were the most agonizing hours of his life, until he saw Marcia's building up ahead. He swerved around cars, missing vehicles by inches. He abruptly stopped his car in the middle of the road, not caring about anything except finding Marcia. He jumped out of the vehicle and ran to her door, then buzzed the button repeatedly, but there was no answer. He pounded on the red door.

"Marcia, please open the door," he said loudly as he shifted his weight from one foot to another. No answer. He knocked again.

"Marcia, please, I'm sorry. I love you. Please open the door," he yelled. He gripped the handle of the door, but it was locked. He looked up at her window.

Suddenly the door flew open, and a lady appeared.

"She not home. She left early this morning," the older woman said to him. He took a few steps toward her, and his heart began to race.

"Madame, do you know where she went? I need to find her. It's urgent."

"Are you Stephane LaRoche?" she asked him.

Stephane nodded, puzzled. He watched as she placed her hand into her pocket and retrieved an envelope, handing it to him.

"Marcia asked me to give you this letter if you came by," she said.

Stephane took the envelope from her. It was addressed to him. "Thank you," he said.

The woman gave him a weak smile, then walked away from him. Stephane's mouth became dry. It was Marcia's handwriting on the envelope. He quickly opened the letter. His hands began to tremble, and his heart hammered in his chest as a wave of nausea invaded him. It read:

My dearest Stephane,

I never wanted to cause you any pain. You are the sweetest, most caring man I have ever met in my life, and you altered my life forever. I have never loved anyone as much as I loved you, and I never will again. I thought we could have a future together, but as you now know, my past came back to haunt me and destroyed everything. I cannot change what happened in my early years. I did what I needed to do to survive at that moment. I will be long gone by the time you receive this letter, so don't bother trying to find me. There is one more thing you need to know before I return home to America: I'm pregnant with your child. I will love and protect this baby with all of my heart. Do not worry or try to find me. We will be fine. I'm so sorry you had to find out this way. Please forgive me. I will love you forever.

– Marcia

Stephane dropped to his knees as his heart shattered into a million pieces. The letter fell from his hands. He lifted his head toward the sky, and a howling scream came out of him. He wept uncontrollably as memories of Marcia flashed in his mind. Finally, he regained his self-control, stood, and wiped his tears away.

"I'm going to find you, even if it's the last thing I do. I love you, Marcia," he said out loud, then walked away.

Acknowledgments

To my fans I would like to thank you for patiently waiting for this novel and for spreading the word about my books. To my children Fouad, Badih, and Amiranour, you bring me joy every day, thank you for all the encouragement during my writing. To a special friend, Steve Cahill in London, England, thank you for being so enthusiastic about helping me with my ending. To Jacqueline Finlay and Patricia Leblanc, thank you for your support and friendship. May we continue to travel so I can get inspired by new destinations.

About the Author

Ann El-Nemr has been writing for five years and this is her sixth novel. She resides in Shrewsbury, Massachusetts. She loves to travel and explore new cities. She loves spending time with her friends and family. Her other published books are *Betrayed*, *Forgiven*, *Lonesome Vagabond*, *The Pledge*, and *Blinded by Obsession*. Ann El-Nemr can be reached on Facebook, Instagram, LinkedIn, www.annelnemr.com, and www.jancarolpublishing.com

Coming Soon

The saga of Marcia and Stephane continues in the next book, *Love, Guilt, Redemption*. Stephane searches for Marcia and his child in the United States only to discover that she is engaged! How will Stephane convince Marcia he still loves her before she marries someone else? Will Marcia's fiancé prevent her from going back to Stephane? Find out in the romantic sequel. Does it have a happy ending?

CPSIA information can be obtained
at www.ICGtesting.com
Printed in the USA
FSHW020647180220

9 781950 895267